Chapter 1

"I'm so nervous" I whisper to myself as I am watching show unfold before me, even though everything seems to be running smoothly. Everyone seems to be enjoying the music, the light sequence for the show is going perfectly, the models are here, the clothes fit but more importantly not one of them has tripped over as they strut the runway (which was my worst fear) because if that happened then that is what people would remember and nothing else. Fashion editors, stylists, celebrities, journalists, and a few WAGs even turned up, dressed head to toe in designer couture, easily wearing outfits that cost at least 5 figures, not including the jewellery they're wearing. They are sitting in a row of white chairs down each side of the runway, legs crossed and no facial expression at all. Photographers are constantly clicking and snapping their cameras, trying to get the perfect shot of the models wearing the latest collection. I notice from backstage that a few of my front row guests are wearing sunglasses which when I think about it is a really good idea as the constant flash of the cameras would be annoying to cope with.

I am hiding behind a giant screen at the start of the runway, where no one can see me. I've been here since the show started. I am counting down the models so I know when I have to go out and take my walk out of the runway at the end of the show. I have 20 models. As I am counting, the closer I am to 20, the more and more nervous I am getting.

"12…13…14"

Everyone does seem to be loving the clothes. The cameras are still flashing so that's got to be a good sign because they wouldn't want to take photos of clothes they didn't want to feature in their magazine or websites…would they?

"15…16…17" I counted quietly but the music was so loud I doubt anyone could hear me even if I was shouting.

As each model walks back towards me, they smile at me, they know how much this means to me and even though they are not saying it i'd like to think that they are proud of me.

"18…19". This is it, one more model to go and then it's my big moment. The last model gets ready to take her strut down the runway, she takes a deep breath then starts strutting. She is wearing this fabulous black belted blazer dress paired with leather, red blood boots with a 5 inch heel that go all the way up to her knees, she is naturally tanned, her black hair is in a neat bun, carrying a clutch bag that matches the boots perfectly. She looks amazing, all the models do. She makes her way towards me, my mouth is so dry I can barely speak, she smiles at me as she makes her way backstage. The lights go dim, the music goes quiet, the crowd goes silent, only for a few seconds. I wait, holding on to these precious seconds before I have to go out there and face all of them on my own. I close my eyes, just savouring these moments. Part of me wants to go out there but there is another part of me that really doesn't want to. What if they didn't like the show? What if when I walk out there they start booing me or throw things at me? What if I go out there and I fall over? Before I have time to think of any more worst case scenarios the lights come back on and I know that my time to walk out there is upon me. I take one final deep breath and make my way out from behind the screen. As soon as they notice me they all stand up and to my amazement they start applauding me. I actually can't believe it, they enjoyed the show and they love the collection. All of that worrying was for nothing, all the worst case scenarios I was having merely seconds ago just faded away. I stand on the runway, taking it all in, the applause, the cheering, the smiles, I turn around and see the models are still wearing their outfits created by me, clapping for me. I can't believe it, this is actually happening to me.

I'm about to turn and walk back down the runway when I notice someone in the back of the room, near the door, a man in a suit. At first I thought I was seeing things but the man started walking towards me and then I realised who it is, "no… it can't be?" I whisper to myself "it just cant be." It's my father. What is he doing here? I know I didn't invite him to this. He makes eye contact with me, I try to walk off the runway but it's like my legs are frozen.

I can't move, no one else in the room has even noticed that anything is wrong, they are still applauding me. I try screaming but it's no use. It's like my whole body is frozen, like I am trapped in my own body, I want to scream and run but my body is not letting me do anything. He is getting closer and closer to me, his familiar frame is more clear to me now, the smart black suit with his signature dark purple tie because he thinks that purple is a sophisticated colour to wear. He's not broken eye contact, I can see he's angry, I can really see his dark green eyes when he's angry. He looks at me, I can't move anywhere, I'm breathing more heavily now, I feel weak like I'm going to faint. Without a moment's warning the lights go out but there is a single light beaming down on my dad and me on the runway, all I can see is blackness where the crowd who moments ago were clapping and cheering me on and now everyone has disappeared and it's silent. I try again to scream to get anyones attention, for someone to come and help me, save me but it's no good. My dad is being silent, not making any noise, he just stares at me with this angry expression on his face. I have never seen him this angry before.

I stand there, not knowing what he is going to do, if he does anything at all, I have no idea if he will shout, scream, will he turn violent and hit me? I stare at him for a few more seconds when suddenly I hear a noise coming from the darkness. The noise sounds familiar, like a ringing noise but I can't remember where I know it from, it's getting louder and louder. My dad is just staring at me, if I couldn't see him breathing I would have thought it was a statue but he's not looking around to see what the noise is so does that mean he can't hear it or he simply doesn't care about the noise. The ringing is getting louder and louder, it's too loud, where is it coming from? I'm getting light headed. I feel so weak, the ground underneath my feet is moving but my legs are still, I feel ... .hot ... .I... .can't ... .breathe.....

Chapter 2

I wake up and gasp for breath and even though I have had the same dream since I can remember, my heart still beats so fast in my chest when I wake up. I look around at the familiar surroundings, the dark blue duvet with my white blanket that I've had since I was a baby, the set of drawers that stand on the other side of the room with the second draw that has never been able to close all the way. A picture of my mother on my bedside table, smiling at me. I turned off my alarm that was ringing next to me and ringing in my dream.

I get out of bed without getting changed, I'm only wearing a plain white t-shirt and a pair of black shorts. I can't hear anyone or any sounds coming from downstairs which means that my dad is at work while my brothers are at football practice before school. They had practice every Friday before school and every Saturday morning which meant that I had the house all to myself two mornings a week and it was heaven.

I make my way to the kitchen but as I am at the top of the stairs I hear a quiet noise, like someone is in the house. I lean over the bannister to see if I can see anyone but I can't see that far ahead into the kitchen. I walk down the stairs very quietly but as I near the bottom I realise that it's quiet…too quiet. I turn the corner to walk into the kitchen and the next thing I know I'm being pushed with a great force into my stomach and then my back hits the wall behind me, my head tilts back and I smack my head also. I'm on the floor holding my head, it feels like it's got its own heartbeat. The pain is getting worse and then I hear two voices laughing, the same two voices that are always laughing at my expense.

"Come on, get up. It aint that bad." I hear Leo, my brother say.

"I barely touched him" I hear my other brother Liam reply.

I would like to say that this is the first time that anything like this has happened but that would be lying, in fact this is getting more and more of a daily occurrence. They think that if they bully me enough it will make me more like them but it won't.

I struggle to stand up but I manage to make it to the table where they are all sitting. I look around the glass table, watching my brothers eating their breakfast, it reminds me of the time I watched a lion devour an antelope, the food barely touched the sides of their mouth and there opposite me was my dad, wearing a crisp white shirt with his famous purple tie, I don't think I had seen him wear any other colour of tie.

"I thought you had work today." I ask, trying not to cry out in pain.

"I have a meeting at 10 with a new DJ." he replied not even looking up from his newspaper.

My dad owns one of the most popular nightclubs in London named Danse which is French for dance. It was my mothers idea to call it something French so it would stand out from the other nightclubs and she was right.

My dad had invested everything he had into making the nightclub a success, he saved every penny he had and put it into the place, he spent the money that his own father left him in his will, he left his job at the bank where he had worked for 8 years. I will never forget my dad's face when he came home from the bank on his last day. He was so happy he bought my mum a huge bunch of roses. He bought me and my brothers a toy car each and when you're 8 years old, that is the best present in the world.

The club was doing really well, hired the right DJs, celebrities would make guest appearances, private parties were being held there, it all seemed to be working out for my dad and his dream but back at home things were not so great.

It all started one friday night, my mum was at home, dad was at the club, I remember sitting at the table, my brothers were playing in the other room. Mum was washing up, she was wearing a light pink dress which looked amazing, my dad always said that no matter what she wore, she always looked amazing. She was a tall woman, not athletic but slim.

I was drawing at the kitchen table, when I heard a loud crash. I looked over at where my mum was standing but she wasn't there. I couldn't see anything, the kitchen island was blocking my view. I got up to look around the island and there she was on the floor, shaking, her eyes had rolled back in her head, all I could see was white, no pupils. I screamed but my brothers who were now fighting in the next room didn't hear me. Just then I heard the front door open, my dad had come back, he had forgotten his phone, he was always forgetting it but today I was glad he had forgotten it.

"What have you done?" He shouted as he ran into the kitchen. He looked so angry with me, like it was my fault.

"Nothing…I…I was" I tried to explain.

"Just shut up and go in there with your brothers and don't come out until I say so." He ordered me.

The next thing I remember is seeing the blue flashing light outside my house, the worried look on my dad's face as they took my mother into the back of the ambulance. All the neighbours are out in their dressing gowns and pyjamas to see what is going on. Mrs Bakewell, who lived next door to us, looked after us that night. She was a small woman, mid 70s, thick framed glasses and she always smelt like mints. My brothers went back to playing while I just stared out the window waiting for them to come back.

After a few days my dad came back and told us that mum has got to stay in hospital for a while, he explained as best as he could what was wrong with her. "Mum is still in the hospital, she has got a headache and the doctors are making her better."

But she never got better and the next six months were the worst, my mother's health deteriorated fast. My father wanted her to die at home, surrounded by her loved ones. Neighbours would come by all the time with either flowers for my mum or a meal of some sort for my dad to heat up for when he didn't feel like cooking which was most of the time. The room for my mum was full of cards, flowers and gifts from family and friends. She was asleep for most of the time but when she was awake and talking her voice was raspy, she always had a soft voice before she was ill. I heard her speak to one of the private nurses that came by the house once and I thought it was a different person, it just didn't sound like her anymore.

It will be 8 years this October and dad still doesn't like to talk about her, he doesn't even like to talk about the memories we shared before the tumour, it's like she never existed. All photos are now in the attic, not destroyed but put out the way, he did that the day after her funeral. If one of us even spoke about her or even said "mum" he would get mad at us.

On the anniversary of her death and her birthday, we never see my dad. He wakes up early and doesn't come home until later, sometimes even the next day, it's like he tries to miss it completely and that's how it's been for the past 8 years.

Since my mum died, he's had a few dates over the years but they were nothing serious, the last date he had was about 3 years ago but since then nothing. The women he dated only liked him because he was the silver fox who owned the fancy nightclub, they were never interested in him, just what he could do for them. They were just a distraction for him and after a date or two, it would just fizzle out.

The nightclub was my dad's pride and joy, a place where he could always escape to if he ever needed to, which was often when my mum died. It was located about 10 minutes from our house so he was never too far away. Me and my brothers could always go and see him whenever we liked. The security guards would let us right in, the people waiting outside would be so confused as they would let us right in but they had to wait outside. I remember one time when I was about fourteen. I was walking home from a friend's house who lived not too far away from my house when I suddenly realised that I left my house key at home so I had to borrow my dads key to get in so I walked right up to the door of the club, saw the long line of people waiting to get in. Frank, who was the bouncer on shift that night, greeted me. "Is my dad in?" I asked but I knew he would be here. "Yeah he's in his office." Frank's voice was so deep but it suited him, he was a tall, stocky man, not a single hair on his head but I just think that added to his character.

"ok, is it alright if i just get my house key from him, I left mine at home and both my brothers are at football practice for another hour?" I explained the situation to him.

"Yeah sure, go right up." he says before un-clipping the velvet rope across the door.

" Is this some kind of joke?" I heard one of the men who was waiting in line. A few of the other people were grumbling and moaning about the situation.

Frank turned to him. "Not that it's any of your business but this is Mike's son."

"And who is mike?" the man replied confused.

"The owner of this club." Frank replied and let me in. "Go on through Jake."

We knew that we weren't allowed to go to the club part, that was off limits to us but we could go to his office and stay there. My father's office was above the nightclub. He had a window that overlooked the whole club, he designed it that way. People could dance and drink and if they looked above the VIP tables, they would see him, on his laptop working, having a meeting or he would be in his white leather chair looking out and watching the people enjoying themselves. Of course he had cameras and security but he always felt like he owed the people in his club that they were safe whilst they had a good time. As he looked over the club, he would often speak to us young boys about the importance of business and how every man needs to have a business of his own, something he has built with his own two hands, something he has total control over. Working for someone else is fine but it can't be permanent. That is what we were taught from a young age by him. It was my fathers dream for all his sons to go to business school and then one day when the time came to take over the club so he could retire knowing that his nightclub was in safe hands so how could I tell him that at least for me his dream wouldn't come true. I didn't want to go to business school and then one day own one third of a nightclub no matter how successful it was. I wanted to study fashion and design and I had already been accepted for an apprenticeship by Roxy Red, the CEO of the house of red, one of the most prestigious fashion houses in the world.

Chapter 3

I remember the first time I ever saw a fashion magazine. I was about 5 years old, my mother had a stack of them all piled up on the living room table. I remember seeing the cover, a strong female model with a serious expression on her face, she was looking away from the camera, her eyes were dark with makeup and she was wearing a silver floor length gown. I didn't care for the articles much but the photographs were mesmerising. Every page was different from the last. Pictures of these strong confident women, all in stunning locations, beach scenes to rooftop views, there was a little bit of everything and every photo was just so well taken, the light really caught the model in a way that somehow made the photo feel like you were there with them on top of a new york rooftop, looking over central park. I think that this was what first interested me about fashion, the clothes were amazing but more than that, it made these women look and feel strong, like they could take on the world and they could do it in a pair of heels.

When I was 8 my mother and I went shopping. I loved this time where it was just us two, I felt at ease whenever I was around her. She was trying on dresses for an event at the club, a singer was having a party at the club and my mum thought that was a good enough reason to buy a new dress, like she needed a reason to buy another dress. She was already wearing this floor length dark blue silk dress when she saw out of the corner of her eye another dress. This dress was different but it was amazing, a short, backless, white dress, it was simple but elegant.
"Which one do you prefer?" she asked me in her soft voice.

I looked at both of them and no matter what I picked, she would have looked amazing in both of them.

"That one." I pointed to the blue silk dress she was already wearing.

"Me too." she smiled which made me smile.

I loved this time with her but the time went by so fast. I wish that the time I spent with my dad and brothers went by as fast. I remember one Thursday night, it was raining and it was in the middle of October and my father took me and my brothers to a football match. It was horrible, not just the weather but the whole experience was one that I never want to go through again. I was sceptical when he mentioned it but I went anyway. To this day I still don't know why I did that. As soon as we sat down I knew I made a bad decision, the weather, the noise, the smell of wet grass. I didn't know when to cheer or even who we were cheering for so in the end I just stayed silent. The only time I spoke was to ask my dad when we could leave.

"Dad, it's cold, can we go home?" He couldn't hear me over the crowd booing because the other team had just scored.

My brothers who were sitting next to me and had better hearing heard what I had asked. "Shut up, we're enjoying it here!"

"But I'm cold."

"We don't care, now shut up."

My dad finally turned to us. "What's going on?"

"I'm cold, can we go home?" I asked before my brothers could say anything."

"In a minute" he says without looking away from the match.

I endured a few more minutes but the cold was making it seem like hours.

I tried to like football but it really wasn't for me, both watching it and playing it, at least when you are watching it and you get bored you can always turn over and watch something else but playing it was a different story. When my brothers and I were in primary school my dad signed us all up for the school football team and both of my brothers took to it like ducks to water, scoring goals and winning trophies but for me, it was not like that and after a few weeks the coach of the team said to my dad that I wasn't "reaching my potential" which means I'm rubbish and the coach wants me off the team. I didn't argue, I was just happy to be off the team and I could finally sleep in on a Saturday morning.

I couldn't take it any longer because the cold was getting bitter. "Dad I'm cold, can we please go?" I pleaded.

"In a minute" he snapped back, this time he looked at me.

He turned back to watch the match. I didn't want to say it again but if I didn't then we would stay here until the end and I couldn't wait that long.

"But dad, I'm cold."

"RIGHT, GET UP!!" he yelled, holding the top of my arm tight. A few people looked over to see what was going on.

"Come on boys, get up we're leaving." he said to my brothers, still grabbing my arm.

"But dad can we just…"

"No, we're leaving, let's go." he interrupted them.

The car journey home I was silent in the back seat while my dad was shouting at me whilst driving. "I can't believe you Jake, you're so selfish, ruining your brothers and mine fun just because you were cold, it wasn't even that cold. When we get home you're going straight to your room, no television or anything. Do I make myself clear?" he shouted, looking at me through the mirror.

I just nodded yes.

My father went quiet for the rest of the journey, my brothers didn't speak either just in case he would yell at them too.

I was sitting in the middle of my two brothers in the back of the car. Leo turned and whispered in my ear "Just you wait until we get home"

"We are going to teach you a lesson" Liam followed on, still quiet so our dad wouldn't hear their threats. They both grinned at each other and then faced forward. I didn't know what was going to happen but all I know is that they would make me pay for making them miss their football match and it would hurt.

I rushed upstairs as fast as I could but it was no use, I wasn't as fast as they were. My father went in the other direction to the living room probably to pour himself a drink while I darted up the stairs but they caught me before I reached the top. They punched me in the stomach with some force and I collapsed, I felt sick. Leo grabbed one of my arms and Liam the other and dragged me along the carpet towards the cupboard where we kept all the bedding and towels, they swung the door open and pulled me inside, they let me go but before I could get up, they slammed the door and were leaning against it from the outside so I couldn't get out.

"Scream all you want, you know that on one will come and save you even if you did." They both taunted me through the door. I wish what they were saying wasn't true but it was. My dad never got involved when I was getting bullied, not once. I have only ever asked for his help once and all he said to me was " stop moaning, it will toughen you up, boys are not meant to cry." So after that I never asked for his help again and I would like to say I never cried but that isn't true but I made sure that he never saw me cry again.

There was enough room in there for me to lie down, my stomach, back and the back of my head were throbbing but I tried not to make a sound and hoped that if I stayed quiet eventually they would get bored, leave the door so I could get out, which they did…eventually.

I started to walk to my father's home office from my bedroom. I don't know why he needed a home office when he already had an office at the club but it wasn't any of my business so I never questioned him. I had the acceptance letter in my hand, ready to show him, if I didn't do it now I never will and then I would spend the rest of my life running a nightclub with two other people who don't want me to be a part of it just as much as I don't want to be a part of it. I just wish that I had told him a few weeks ago when I first got the acceptance letter.

There were so many opportunities I could have told him my plans but at the last second I couldn't do it, I lost my confidence. I could have told him over breakfast a few days ago when it was just the two of us, he was reading the paper.

"Dad"

"What" he replied, not looking up from his paper.

"I… I …" I started to stutter, then my courage had gone so I just said "I need some milk, could you pass me the milk please" which he did, still not looking up from his paper.

I could have told him when he took me to school yesterday and it was just the two of us. "Dad I need to tell you something"

"What?"

"I… I …" my confidence had left me yet again so I just said the first thing that came to me so I wouldn't look strange.

"I need you to drop me off here today"

"Ok" he pulled over, confused at my request.

I had to tell him soon because in a few days I will be leaving for the apprenticeship. Whatever was going to happen I wasn't going to find out if I just stood here. I was just about to knock on the door when my brothers pushed me into the wall as they snatched the letter out of my hand.

"What's this then?" Leo asked me, holding my letter to the light.

"It's personal." I replied.

"Who could be writing to you, you have no friends" Liam said with a laugh.

Without another word they took the piece of paper out the envelope and began to read. I would have loved to run up, snatch it from them but if my past experiences have taught me anything it's that when I try and get something back from them, it never works out well for me so now I don't even bother.

"What's this all about?" Leo asked.

"It's nothing," I replied. They both looked confused as they read the letter.

"Well it looks like you have been accepted as an apprenticeship for a fashion company".

It's not like I could lie, it's right there in black and white so I just stayed silent.

"So does dad know about this." Leo asked but still looking at the letter.

I was apprehensive about saying "no" because I knew that as soon as I did, they would both tell him anyway and then my secret would be out. "No he doesn't" I finally uttered.

"Interesting," he replied. Liam and Leo both look at each other, smiled, they pushed past me with some force, knocking me to the ground

Chapter 4

I staggered to my feet, the door was closed to my father's office but I could hear voices from the other side. I opened the door I saw my dad standing behind his desk, holding the letter in his hand, my brothers are standing nearby smirking, they always like getting me into trouble or they loved finding new ways for my dad to be disappointed in me in some way so when they saw that letter all they saw was another opportunity for my dad to look at me with shame.

"Can you guys give us a minute?" without saying anything they left. I know that they wanted to stay and hear the conversation but they knew that if they had tried to convince my dad to stay in the room then they would have got shouted at so they left but not before smiling at me as they walked past me. A few seconds later I heard the office door shut.

He stares at me for a few seconds before saying anything. I feel uneasy when he doesn't speak, he's just staring, the only noise that I can hear is the fire cracking in the distance.

"So what is this all about ?" he holds the letter up in his left hand. Didn't know how to explain what it was, how much did he know or not know so I decided to tell the truth and accept my punishment whatever it may be. "It's my acceptance letter from a fashion house. I got accepted into their apprenticeship program. I will start in a few days."

As soon as I said it, it was like a huge weight had been lifted from my shoulders. I had finally told my dad about the apprenticeship. He didn't say anything for what felt like an eternity but in reality was about 10 seconds.

"Absolutely not!" he said with a raised voice.

"Wha…Why?"

"Because I said so, I will not have one of my sons making dresses for a living. I will be humiliated, if people found out about this, this could ruin me and the reputation that I have spent so many years building."

"But this is something I really want to do." I pleaded with him.

"I don't care, you are going to call them right now and tell them that you're not taking the placement and they should give it to someone else." he takes his phone out his back pocket, dials the number that is on the letter.

"Please dad, don't make me do this." I can feel tears forcing their way to my eyes. He's not listening, he holds out the phone to me, it's ringing. My dad stares at me until I take the phone out of his hand and I put it to my ear.

"Hello house of red, Ester speaking, how can I help you?" Her voice is loud but not annoying.

"Hi, this is Jake Silver…"

"Oh yes, Jake Silver, yes we have got you down to start your apprenticeship on the 12th." She interrupts me but I don't mind.

"Yes, that's it but…" I stop talking and look at my dad, hoping he would stop me but he doesn't. He just keeps staring at me, waiting for me to finish on the phone. "I'm sorry but I can't…I can't accept the placement" I can feel tears rising.

"Oh no, I'm sorry to hear that, are you sure?" she asks, sounding concerned.

I look at my dad for the final time, wishing he would stop me but he just stands there looking at me.

"Yeah I'm sure." I replied.

"Well I hope that you enjoy the apprenticeship that you did accept and I wish you all the best." Ester sounded so happy that she has no idea that the person she is talking to is about to cry on the other end of the line

"Thank you." I say, trying not to cry.

"Bye."

"Bye." I ended the call. My dad put the phone back in his pocket before sitting back in his chair. "Now that is all taken care of, I have got actual business to be getting on with so will you close the door on your way out." He is talking like nothing has happened, like he hasn't just killed my dream about working for one of the biggest fashion houses in the country. I walk out the office, I get to the door and I realise that I need to say something or if I don't this will eat me alive for the rest of my life.

"I DON'T WANT TO RUN A STUPID NIGHTCLUB!!!" I scream at him. I have never done that before in my life, even when I have been mad, I have never screamed like that before but a small part of me likes it, like I had finally found my voice. My dads eyes are so angry, it's like they are looking right through my soul.

"STUPID NIGHTCLUB!!!" he shouted, getting up from his seat and making his way around his desk. "Well if it wasn't for this stupid nightclub, we wouldn't have this nice house, you wouldn't go to a nice school or you wouldn't have any of the nice things that you do!" He was standing right in front of me, his nose just inches away from mine, I could smell his breath as he shouted at me, it smelled like stale coffee."You owe the life you have to this "stupid nightclub." I have really angered him. "I have put everything I have into this nightclub, I have made it a success." he took a few steps toward his desk. "Exactly, YOU have put everything into it, not me!" I exclaim. "Surely I should be allowed to do the same thing with something I care about rather than something I don't." I suggest.

"No son of mine is going to be making dresses for a living" that phrase hung in the air for a few seconds, not breaking eye contact. "Fine" I walk past him to grab the letter that is still flat on his desk. He sees that I am going to grab the letter, he grabs my arm before I have time to reach it.

"What do you think you're doing?" He talks.

"Getting the letter and ringing them back."

"You're not having the letter"

"Yes I am." I attempted to grab the letter out of his hand, just like that his right hand smacked me in the face, I fell back.

I landed on the black leather sofa which was behind me. I wish that could say that this was the first time he has ever hit me but that would be a lie. The first time he hit me I was about 11 and I had a poster on my bedroom wall of a model, she was wearing a pink floor length gown in the middle of the desert, she had this strong expression on her face, she was wearing dark eyeshadow and her hair was down with loose curls. It wasn't a very big poster but when my dad saw it he went mad, hit me and ripped down all my posters, every single one of them. I remember being really confused because my dad had no problem with my brothers having posters up in their room of football players or singers so I never understood why they were allowed to and I wasn't. I got told to "never put these sort of pictures on my wall again." and we never spoke of it after that.

My eyesight went blurry as I lifted my head up, the room was spinning. He was standing next to the fire. "This is for your own good" he uttered and then he placed the letter in the fire. I watched the letter slowly burn, he just stood there until it was unsaveable then went back to his desk. My head was throbbing but my eyes were coming back into focus. I slowly rose from the sofa, ignoring my pain in my head. I didn't even look back at him, my eye felt like it had its own heartbeat. I managed to get to my room, and I can see that my bedroom door is open a little. I push it all the way open, my room is a mess, clothes out of my wardrobe are on the floor, my draws are all open, even my bin which was mostly full of scrap bits of paper were all over the floor.

I'm looking around for my folder, the folder that has all my designs in it, the one I was going to take with me to my apprenticeship. I had been working on them for weeks. I had hid it under my mattress so no one would find it but someone had found it because my mattress had been flipped. I looked under the bed to see if it had fallen down through the base of the bed but it wasn't there. I was starting to panic, I didn't want anything to happen to it. I knelt down looking underneath the clothes and there it was, ripped in half and all the designs were gone, ripped up into pieces buried underneath the clothes. I was in shock. I could feel the tears filling my eyes again. I picked up a piece of one design and a piece of another design and cried.
"What happened in here?" I hear a voice come from the doorway.
"No idea." Leo answers sarcastically.
My brothers have done some horrible things to me in the past but this was by far the worst. I don't even turn to look at them. I don't say anything, I just stay knelt with my ripped designs around me, tears rolling down my cheeks. I can hear them laughing as they walk away.

Chapter 5

Two days had passed by since my dad hit me in his office, we haven't spoken a word since it happened. Which isn't anything strange there, we never really had a lot to say to one another for some time but this incident has made us completely silent to one another. My eye is still swollen and it has turned a dark purple and pink, still hurts to touch. My dad saw it and he just looked away. I think very deep down he was sorry for what had happened but he would never admit it. I don't think my dad has ever uttered the words "I'm sorry" to anyone in his life, whether he was right or wrong.

My brothers gave me more of a reaction when they saw my face.
"Nice makeup" Liam mocked.
"You deserved it" Leo joined in.
"You got let off easy."
They are saying it louder and louder as I'm walking away. I refuse to turn around giving them the reaction that they are so desperately craving.
"Does this mean you're gay now? I hear Leo shout. I will never understand why he said that, "does this mean you're gay now." Just because I prefer to design outfits and read fashion magazines to playing football on a dirty pitch doesn't mean that I am gay, maybe I just like to keep clean and hate getting dirty.
I just stand there, I close my eyes and count to five. Still refusing to turn around. I don't get angry. I just carry on walking upstairs. They have destroyed my folder, the one thing I actually cared about so now

that it's gone, they can't take anything else away from me which makes me feel a bit better.

Saturday mornings are perfect in my house, my dad has already left for work and he won't be home until the early hours of Sunday morning which suits me fine. Both Liam and Leo are out, they have football practice in the morning and then they go out with friends afterwards which usually means that they won't be back until late maybe even the next day, they always manage to find a house party to go to which leaves me alone all Saturday which is perfect for me.

I woke up around 8am on a Saturday morning, I ate my breakfast in peace without being slammed into a wall or without being punched. On Saturdays I always have pancakes. I'm just about to tuck into the stack of blueberry pancakes when I hear the door knock. I quickly put a forkful of pancake in my mouth and headed for the door. I see through the pane of glass on the front door that it's a delivery driver, wearing a red cap and matching jacket.
"Hello" I say as I open the door.
"Parcel for Mike Silver" he replies holding a small box and a pad waiting for me to sign. That's one thing I never understood about delivery drivers, they never say hello, not even hey or hi
I don't say anything, I just grab the pen and pad and sign on the dotted line then close the door.

I look at the parcel. Whatever it is, its light, barely feels like nothing is in the box at all.

Now i'm in a dilemma because my dad told us that if a parcel gets delivered to the house and he's not there then we are to take it to the club and leave it in his office for him no matter what the parcel is we should take it to the club.

Even though I don't want to go and see him after all that has happened, if I don't go then he will probably end up shouting at me again like the other night and I really don't want to go through all that again so I finish off my pancakes that have gone a little cold now, get changed and make my way to the club.

We only live about 10 minutes away from the club, which I was glad about today because there was a chill in the air and I was only wearing a light jacket. By the time I got to the club it was 9am. No matter how many times I had seen the club in the daytime it was still weird seeing it without the lights on, the music on loud and without a lot of people dancing and drinking. There was music playing when I entered but it wasn't loud, the staff were playing music on low and chatting whilst they were getting the place ready for the nighttime. I am just about to walk up the stairs when I hear my name being called from behind me " Jake"

I turn around as I turn to look at the familiar voice. It was Debra Nest, the manager, my dad was the owner but he needed someone to be in charge for when he wasn't there, which was not a lot of the time but

Debra never seemed to mind. My father and Debra had known each other for years so when she lost her job as the manager of a hotel due to the hotel closing down, my dad hired her a few weeks before he opened up Danse and the two of them have gotten along great. She was like part of the family I have known her from birth, she was kind of a second mum to me.

"What have you done to your face?" she asks concerned as she examines my eye, which is still bruised.

"Oh it's my own fault, I fell over the bath and the tap caught my eye." I know that I shouldn't have lied but I just couldn't bring myself to tell her the truth. Debra really looks up to my dad, she owes him a lot, he hired her when no one else would so I just don't want her to think bad of him.

"What are we going to do with you?" she says jokingly.

I laugh hoping we can talk about something else. "Is my dad here?" I ask, trying to change the subject.

"Yeah he's upstairs in his office, you know your dad, always working." she states.

"Ok I'm just going to go and give him this parcel."

"Ok I will see you later" we hug and we go our separate ways.

I walk up to what feels like a thousand steps to his office. As I approach the door I can hear a woman's voice coming from the office. I hear my dads voice as well, it sounds like they are arguing. I stay quiet and see if I can hear what they are saying.

"Just leave my office" I hear my dad tell her.

"Mr Silver, please let me just talk to Jake, see what he has to say about this amazing opportunity I have for him." she replies.

They are arguing about me, what amazing opportunity is she talking about. How does this mystery woman know my name?

"You are not speaking to my son and that is final."

"But this is an amazing opportunity for him."

"I said no, now leave." I could tell by my dads voice he was angry. Without thinking about it I opened the door. My dad is sitting behind his desk and the mystery woman has her back towards me. She has long blonde hair and is wearing a blood red blazer with matching trousers with a pair of black heels.

"Get out!" my dad orders me.

"I heard my name, who's this?" I walk around to see the mystery woman's face and then I know who she is. "You're ….you're Roxy Red" I stuttered.

"You must be Jake, it's such a pleasure to meet you" she stands up to shake my hand. She is a tall woman, even without the heels.

"I can't believe it's you. I have been following your work for years, what are you doing here?" I ask her.

"She was just leaving." My dad speaks before she has a chance to reply. She waits for a few seconds so she knows that he is done talking and then replies.

"I'm here to see if I could change your mind about the apprenticeship, honestly Jake, your designs that you submitted are amazing and I had to meet the person who designed them" I smile. Roxy Red, the woman who owns one of the biggest fashion houses in the world is praising me for my designs. "But then I was told that you had passed on the apprenticeship and no longer wanted to do it so I wanted to see if I could change your mind, hoping you would reconsider."

"Well he doesn't." my dad answered.

"I didn't ask you, did I." She looked at my dad like she wanted to slap him and I wouldnt of blamed her if she did. My dad hated anyone who stood up to him, he was not used to it. "Here" she takes a card from her bag. "Why don't you think about it and give me a call if you change your mind." She picks up her bag off the floor and walks out the office without looking back at my dad.

"Well he won't" he yells as she closes the office door, I can hear her heels click, get fainter and fainter as she walks away.

It is silent in the office for a few seconds, I'm facing the door, my dad is still at his desk, he must be sitting now as I can't hear him moving behind me. I turn around, he's reading a bunch of papers that are filling his desk.

"Why won't you let me do this apprenticeship?" I finally said after watching him for a few seconds.

"I've already told you, no son of mine is going to be making dresses for a living" his tone of voice is so bitter, like just the thought of me designing clothes for a living makes him physically sick.

"Don't you want me to do something that actually makes me happy rather than do something that makes you happy." I state.

"This club will make you happy… one day"

"No it wont, I don't want to run this place with two people who hate me so much that they will use this place to torture me in new ways."

"What you talking about your brothers don't torture you." he scoffs.

"Do you not live in the same house I do because every opportunity they get, they will take it to bully me in some way." I speak, trying not to cry but I can already feel my throat get tight and my eyes start filling up. My bruised eye is starting to sting.

"That's just boys being boys, you know what your problem is? You're just too sensitive and you need to toughen up a little." That phrase stays in the air for about 10 seconds before I can respond. I hate when he tells me that I'm just too sensitive and that I should toughen up. I have heard that same line over and over again since I was little. It's like he says it to justify my brothers bullying me just so he hasn't got to punish them.

I can feel the anger burning up inside me, it's like something inside of me has snapped, suddenly I remember all the hits both verbally and physically, it's like someone had captured it on video and was showing it to me and only me. All the time I was locked in a dark room by my brothers, me telling my dad but he didn't want to know, the time they pushed me down the stairs on my birthday just because they could, when my dad saw me lying at the bottom of the stairs, he told me "to just walk it off." Every time they hit me in the car for just being there and then when my dad would look back at us they would act like they had done nothing wrong. The day my dad ripped the posters off my bedroom wall of all the fashion models, the anger in his eyes as he was doing it, a memory I will never forget unfortunately. My brothers when they trashed my room, my folder of all my designs ripped to pieces. The day my dad hit me in his office, I remember feeling sick when I hit the sofa. I knew that I couldn't carry on living this way.

"NO… NO…NO!!!" I shout. He looks up from the papers he's reading at his desk "NO I AM NOT TOO SENSITIVE AND I DON'T NEED TO TOUGHEN UP!" I threw the small box that I am still carrying at him. I feel this huge weight has been lifted off my shoulders, it's like all that anger that has been building up for so long has finally left my body and I feel so much better because of it.

"You better watch that tone of yours." he says, not raising his voice. He looks at me from across the room like he wants to say something more but he either doesn't know what to say or he doesn't know how to put it together in a sentence.

"I'm going to do this apprenticeship and there is nothing you can do about it." I say before he has time to say anything.

He sits there for a minute then he gets up out of his seat and slowly makes his way over to where I am standing. "You think I am going to let you do this and embarrass me in this manner, then you have got another thing coming." he says, still walking over to me. I don't know what he will do, he can hit me again but I have so much adrenaline going through me right now I really don't care. I have made up my mind.

"I'm going to do it and you can't stop me." I tell him, I am inches away from his face, I can smell the coffee he had earlier that day. "You leave that door, don't even think about coming back." I grabbed the handle "just remember one thing, I gave you everything you have and I can take it away from you just as easily."

He stared at me while I stood there and thought about the last part, he had given me everything in my life up to that point but then I started to think about all the things he hadn't given me, the important things, things that money can't buy, patience, time, support and the most important one of all love. At that moment I knew that if I didn't leave now I never would and then I would never be free of him.

Without thinking about it, I pulled on the handle and left, running down the stairs. I could hear Debra call after me but I ran so fast and I wasn't going to turn back so I just carried on running. I didn't stop until I got to my house. I called Roxy from the card she had given me. I dialled the number, my hands were shaking, I waited for someone to answer, I thought about everything that had just happened to me in the last hour and how my life would turn out now that I was all on my own.

"Hello."

Chapter 6

A few hours later I was outside my house with a suitcase full of the remainder of my clothes that my brothers had not damaged in some way. I can't believe this is happening to me. A few hours ago I was walking to my dad's nightclub to drop off a parcel which I actually threw at the wall and now my suitcase is packed and I'm ready to start my fashion apprenticeship. I feel so nervous, every time I see a car go by I think that it is Roxy's car but when it passes my nerves subside but then they start up again when I see the next car. After giving her my address, she told me to meet her outside my house at 6pm. The reason why I picked that particular hour is I know for certain that no one would be home for at least another hour. That would be the last thing I want is to run into my brothers or worse my dad whilst I was trying to leave so this way I can avoid them all.

I checked my phone, it read 5.57pm. I sat down on the steps that lead up to the front door, another car drives past but it's not her. I don't know what car I am looking for, I should have asked when I was on the phone but I completely forgot. No one is out tonight, no couples walking by, no one walking their dog, no one out jogging, it's like I have the whole street to myself. There is a slight breeze tonight which hurts my eye when I face the direction the wind is blowing. Another car drives past but it just keeps going. I look at my phone again, 5.58pm it reads. I didn't have any dinner, I was too excited about the apprenticeship and everything that entails that I was too excited about food, maybe I can get something later. I see a car driving slowly down the street, a black limo, even though I live in a nice area of London, even people around here don't just have a limo that takes them places,

I knew this was her. It pulls up right in front of me, the window descends and there she is looking stunning as ever, not a hair out of place, natural makeup which really complements her face.

"You ready." she asks as the top on the window stops just below her face.

I took a look behind me at the house where I had lived for the majority of my life, all the memories I had had in that place. When my mum was alive there were some good times but when she died and after I can't recall many good times after that. I turned to face Roxy who was smiling at me. "I'm ready." I replied.

Roxy tells me all that is involved in the apprenticeship. I will have my own room in a house that I will share with 2 other designers. We will learn everything there is to know about how to put a fashion show together and what it involves. Roxy didn't shy away from what would be expected of me, the early mornings and the late nights, she also told me the amount of times her and her team have gone without food just because they were so wrapped up in their work was too numerous to mention and when they did finally managed to grab something to eat, it was 2 o'clock in the morning so they would order a take out which I wouldn't mind. She also informs me that there will be a few parties that I can attend, and meet other designers, models, photographers and other people from the fashion industry which I am so excited about.

I knew from a very early age that even though from the outside, the fashion world might look glamorous with perfect models, with flawless skin, putting on fashion shows that only lasted a few minutes, there was a dark side to it. I had watched so many documentaries about the lives of famous fashion designers and how they came to be, what they went through to get to where they are today and most of it was through hard work and even though they were at the top of the industry, they still had to put in the work which meant early mornings, late nights, not eating properly and suffer setbacks just to put on a 10 minute fashion show.

As she is talking to me I can see that she is looking at my eye. I know that she wants to ask me about it. I'm just about to explain what happened when she asks me, "Can I ask you something?"

"Sure"

"You don't have to tell me but what happened to your eye?" She takes a sip of her champagne.

"My dad, he… he hit me." I didn't want to say it like that but at the same time I'm glad I did say it like that at least I was being honest with her.

"I'm so sorry" she apologised like it was her fault, like she could have done something to stop it from happening.

"It's fine." I say but not convincingly,

"I take it it's not the first time either?" she asks but she already knows that answer.

I just shake my head no.

"Why would he do something like that?" she asks before taking another sip of champagne.

"Because of this apprenticeship."

"What do you mean?" She looks confused by what I have just said.

"Well my dad has never wanted me to take this apprenticeship" I start to explain.

"Yeah I kind of got that from the meeting I had with him earlier." She continued.

"Well I told him that I wanted to do it, we argued and then he hit me and I didn't speak to him until I saw you in his office."

"Why doesn't he want you to do it?"

"When I was younger I told him once how much I wanted to design clothes one day and he turned to me and said that if i did that, he would disown me so for years after that I was so scared about him finding out that I was secretly designing outfits in my room and hiding the designs away but there comes a time when you can't keep hiding anymore." I look out the window, trying to avoid eye contact with her.

"Jake I'm so sorry." she apologised again.

"All I wanted was his approval, just once but I am only just realising that it is never going to happen and I just need to accept it." I say facing her again.

We talk more about different things. I found out a few more things about her that I didn't know before. Firstly her name isn't Roxy Red which doesn't surprise me but I wasn't sure, her real name is Dorothy Polo which she hates and I can sort of see why. The name Roxy comes from when she was on a night out in her early twenties and this guy wanted to buy her a drink and she made him a deal that if he could guess her name then he could buy her a drink, she knew that whatever name he said that is the name she would go along with and he said "Roxy" and the name just stuck with her and the name Red comes from her favourite colour. She has a sister, Gina who is a teacher. They are still close and talk everyday. I envied her in that way. I would love to have that kind of relationship with my brothers, even though our lives have gone down different paths we can still be there for one another but sadly that is just not how it is.

She went to college and university but it wasn't until she went travelling for a year where she fell in love with fashion. Seeing how fashion is different in different countries all over the world so that when she decided that is what she wanted to do, was to be a fashion designer and to create her own line.

The car stops on a random street, newly built two storey houses with a little garden. "We're here." she says as the driver opens the door for her.

"Here, where?" I was confused, looking out the car window and all I could see was a row of newly built houses.

"Your new home." she says as she makes her way to the front door of the house right in front of us.

I looked up at the house, it's so much smaller than I was expecting but I didn't mind. I knew this wasn't my permanent home.

The house was small but modern, a small hallway which had three hooks for coats. The living room to the left, which was decorated in neutral colours, looked like a show home for potential buyers. Living room was cosy, two dark brown sofas with a coffee table in the middle of the room. Tv mounted on the wall and a rug just in front of the electric fireplace. Two sliding doors behind one of the sofas which led into the dining room which had nothing in it but a table and chairs and another door that led to the kitchen.

The kitchen was also small even though there wasn't much in there. Cupboards all the way around, built-in oven, all the major appliances you would need in a new home. The sink looked so new like no one had ever washed a single plate or piece of cutlery in there.

"Shall we go and see your room?" she asked but she was already going up the stairs.

"Sure" I followed her up the stairs which led us to three doors. She opened the furthest one from where we were standing. I looked inside and saw just a single bed, a desk and a wardrobe. Compared to my old room this room was like a shoe box but at least my drawing would be safe in this room and I wouldn't have to worry about them being destroyed.

"Do you like it?" she asked, smiling.

"It's perfect." I wasn't lying but I wasn't telling the whole truth either.

"Good, I'm glad." She genuinely looks so happy that I like it. "These other two doors are just other bedrooms but I wanted you to have the biggest room as you are the first one here." she informs me. My room is the biggest room. I can only imagine what the small room is like if what I am staying in is considered big.

As I look around I notice that something is missing, where is the bathroom? I didn't see it downstairs. "Where is the bathroom?" I am now curious. Please tell me that this house does have a bathroom.

"Oh yeah, it's downstairs, it's off from the kitchen."

"Ok … so when do the others get here?" I ask as I put my suitcase on the bed.

"They will be here soon, the next few days." she smiles. "Right, well I better go. I have got a few things to sort out but I will be back first thing in the morning to pick you up so get some sleep and I will see you tomorrow morning."

As soon as I heard the door closed I ran to the kitchen to see if I could find anything to eat, the only thing that the cupboards had to offer was a packet of pasta and a half a loaf of bread that was now past its sell by date. So I chucked the bread away and started making the pasta. It wasn't much of a meal but I was so hungry and I didn't have a lot of choice.

After dinner I decided to watch a little T.V but there really wasn't much worth watching so I went upstairs to unpack my clothes. I didn't pack everything I owned but I managed to pack a good amount of not just clothes but also belongings. I placed the photo I have of my mum at the side of my bed, she took the photo a few years before she got sick and it's my favourite photo of her, she is sitting in a garden chair with a drink in her hand with pink sunglasses on her head, her smile is so big, it really was her best feature.

I had a shower when I finished packing and got into bed, it had been a very tiring day and now all I wanted to do was to sleep. I put some cream on my eye which was still sensitive to touch. I'm not sure if the cream was working but I still applied it. The bed wasn't comfortable but it was still better than being at home or worse on the streets, here I was safe and warm and that is all that I was bothered about. I lied, staring at the ceiling, thinking about everything, what was my dad going to say when he noticed I had gone, it's not like I left a note for him to find, telling him where I am or even that I left. I don't think he would care anyway. I could feel my eyelids getting heavy and a few seconds later I fell asleep and all the questions and worries I had for the day had gone… for now.

Chapter 7

I woke up the next morning and for a few seconds I didn't know where I was. The unfamiliar surroundings puzzle me then it all comes flooding back to me. Roxy, the apprenticeship, my dad, the pain in my eye. I lie there, looking up at the ceiling, thinking about everything that has happened in the last 24 hours and how my life has changed all because I was brave enough to take a chance on myself.

I made my way downstairs to the kitchen, it was so cold. I hate the cold especially in the morning as I never want to leave my bed. I am looking around the kitchen for something to eat but I can't find anything, no bread to make toast, no cereal or milk. I looked in every cupboard but they were all completely empty. I even looked in the freezer to see if there was anything I could heat up but it was just as bare as the cupboard and fridge. I was thinking about how hungry I was and all I could think about was a nice egg and sausage sandwich when the thought of eating suddenly left my head when I heard a loud knock on the door.

Apart from Roxy, no one knows I am here, until last night I didn't know I would be here so who could be knocking at the door at this time in the morning. The door knocked again, I could feel my heart beat faster. I slowly crept to the front door, trying not to make a sound so as to alert the person on the other side of the door that someone is here.

I put my left eye onto the door viewer only to see it was Roxy standing waiting outside, wearing a dark red coat, her hair down and a pair of sunglasses on, even though the sun wasn't even out. I sighed in relief and opened the door for her.

"Finally I thought I was going to be out there all day" she said as she made her way in.

"Sorry I didn't know it was you" I apologised.

She looked at me up and down, judging what I was wearing. "You're not wearing that today are you?" she asked but I could tell by the tone of her voice that she wasn't asking me she was telling me to get changed.

"Don't worry I'm gonna get changed." I reassured her

"Oh good" she sighed with relief "because you can't meet the team looking like that"

"You mean I'm actually getting to meet the team today" I say excitedly. I have heard that she has a team but I have never seen them, it's like a secret within the fashion world. People have claimed that they have been part of her team but then left due to "creative differences' others say she has had the same team for the last 15 years but they never do interviews or even talk to the press. One newspaper even said that she hired a bunch of mutes to work for her so to actually see for myself the truth behind all the headlines will be interesting.

I was just about to run up the stairs to get changed when I remembered that I was still hungry. "Roxy," I said as I stopped myself on the stairs.

She looked up at me from her phone

"Is there any chance we could get some breakfast, it's just I am starving and there is nothing to eat."

She blinks a few times, looks at me like she is trying to think of something to say "oh ye..yeah" she stutters. " I was meant to tell my assistant to pick up a few things and I completely forgot. I'm sorry but we can pick up some breakfast on the way to the office, my treat."she smiles at me then looks back to her phone. I walked up the rest of the stairs thinking to myself that the whole interaction was a little weird but I was so excited to meet her team that I didn't give it a second thought.

We got breakfast and then made our way to the studio. We had to get a taxi there as Roxy's personal chauffeur was sick but when I asked her about him she didn't look at me once she just kept staring at her phone the entire time. The studio was a large building about a 20 minute drive from the house, from the outside it looked like an abandoned warehouse but Roxy told me that the best designers have their studios in buildings like these so no one knows that they are there, like they are hidden in plain sight. We took the lift up to the 5th floor which opened up to a large room, where there were tables scattered about, sketches and pieces of fabric pinned to boards that were around the room, about 10 people sketching around the large table then rushing to another table to get the other peoples opinion, there was a woman dressed in a floor length black backless dress and another woman at the hemline with a few pins in her hands, the model is looking straight ahead with a serious expression on her face while the seamstress is trying to concentrate on fixing the dress.

"Hi Roxy" she calls out with a pin between her teeth.

"Hey…you." she replies walking past her, not looking her in the eye.

"Who was that?" I ask when we get out of ear shot

"No idea, she isn't that important if I can't remember her name."

It's a bit rude of her to not know the people that work for you but I just put it in the back of my mind, maybe she was new or maybe she just forgot her name.

"Roxy, darling." I heard a posh voice come from behind us. We both turned around and there was a man standing there, about 50, a small beard which was going grey, black thick framed glasses which looked like they had no actual purpose other than decoration. They both kissed each other on the cheek which I never understood the proper etiquette for kissing, is it one kiss each cheek, one kiss on one cheek and that's it. Does it depend on who you're kissing? I had no idea.

"Mario, how are you?" she asked him, smiling.

"Let's not even go there. Firstly the models are being divas, "this isn't MY shade of lipstick, i'm not working with her" that's the kind of drama I have to deal with for the past twelve hours. Secondly the black fabric got delivered today but it was the wrong shade, so now gotta send it back and to make this day even worse, the lady who does my botox has just cancelled my appointment."

"Oh no!" Roxy gasps like this was the worst news in the whole world. "I know, something about her pipe burst at her salon and now she needs to sort it out. What about me? What about my lines? I need to sort these out." he says, touching his face to these invisible lines that no one can see other than him. I don't even think Roxy can see them. I think she is just humouring him.

"Im sorry darling" she sounds so sincere, like she really feels his pain of not having botox injections
"Thank you, anyway, who do we have here?" He looks at me up and down. I could tell that he was judging me just by my appearance and the fact that I have got a black eye doesn't help.
"Sorry, Mario Tork, this is Jake Silver, our new apprentice. Jake, this is Mario, our creative director." Apparently they met when Roxy was 18 and Mario was 22, she was an aspiring model and he was designing clothes but when her career took off and she was flying all over the world, she bought Mario along to meet people in the industry but no one ever gave him the chance that she thought he truly deserved so when she decided to create her first collection and start the House of Red, Mario was her go to guy and rest is history.

I put my hand out to shake it but he just laughs "aww that's sweet but I don't shake hands." he says condescendingly. He and Roxy share a little laugh before he continues. "So…it looks like you have been in the wars, what happened there?"

I really don't like this guy and there is no way I am telling him what happened just so he can look at me with more pity than he already does. "Nothing just walked into a door."

"Sure, I have done that a few times, especially after a few vodkas." He starts to laugh. I know that he doesn't believe me but I don't care.

I met the rest of the team and they weren't so bad, well they were much nicer than Mario. Dylan was another designer who had worked here for about 3 years, about 30, short brown hair, wearing a checked shirt with a bow tie which kinda suited him.

Bridget was Roxys assistant, she had long shiny black hair that ended half way down her back. She was tall enough that she didn't need to wear heels but she did as Roxy instructed her too. She was constantly glued to her phone, always taking a call or replying to emails, on behalf of Roxy.

Katie was the seamstress that Roxy couldn't be bothered to remember her name, late 30s, light brown hair, petite. She was nice, quiet, she just did what she was paid to do then go home, she never got involved in the drama that the models caused and tried to stay out of the way as much as possible.

There were a few other people around but I didn't know their names yet but I'm sure I would get to know each and every single one of them. As I watched them work I kept thinking to myself how grateful I was, standing here in one of the biggest fashion houses in the world, watching all these creative and talented people around me be their true selves, working on something that they are so passionate about and I am a part of this. I will never forget this experience.

Chapter 8

The next couple of days went by so quickly. The daily routine was so gruelling to start with but after about a week I was getting used to the early mornings and the very late nights. We would start the day at 6 in the morning and wouldn't finish until 1 in the morning but that is the price we pay to create a fashion show, not to mention I am learning so much not just about the industry and the dedication that goes into putting on a fashion show but of Roxy herself. I now know that she has her coffee black, no sugar, she hates the colour beige (it's too plain) and she has a birthmark on her hand that looks like a heart which I didn't notice before.

But as for the fashion industry, I was learning a lot. Today was the day we were going to be auditioning models for the upcoming show in a few weeks. I was just going to sit there and watch Roxy pick and choose the models who she thought would be good for the show. I had never seen an audition process take place and now I was going to get a front row seat at one. At least the bruise on my eye had gone down with a little help from Katie the makeup artist and it wasn't so tender anymore to touch. I'm glad it went down before this audition as I didn't want people to be looking and making comments about it.

I was in the car on my way to the audition when I got a call from Roxy.

"Hello." I say, puzzled as to why she is calling me as I am going to see her in the next few minutes.

"Hi darling." she bellowed down the phone, it was too early in the morning to hear her voice that loud "I'm so sorry but I can't make it to the audition." I heard her say. What does she mean she can't make the audition? She was the one who organised it and confirmed it with me last night so what has changed in the last six hours. "Oh so does that mean we have to reschedule or cancel?" I ask hoping that whatever is going on she can get out of it as I am really looking forward to this audition.

"Absolutely not, you will have to do it for me"

"Sorry, what…what did you say?" I stutter. I really hope that she just didn't say what I thought she just said. Me picking out models. ME!!!

"You will have to do the audition by yourself, I am sure that you will pick absolutely gorgeous models for me" she said nonchalantly. Like it was no big deal that she wanted me to pick models for her show

"I …I can't do that." I could barely speak.

"Course you can, just sit there, ask them to walk in front of you and if you like the look of them, tell them they are through to the next round, if not tell them to go home, anyway got to go, speak soon, bye." She hung up before I could say another word.

I just wanted to watch and now it turns out I'm in charge.

Me!!! Judging models.

The car pulls up outside the hotel, I make my way to their conference room for the audition. I walk in and the whole room is full of aspiring models, all chatting away in their groups, all different shapes and sizes, some were wearing casual clothes like jeans and a t-shirt with their hair in a ponytail whilst other were wearing skirts with a blouse and jacket, like they are going to a job interview afterwards. There must have been about 100-150 models here to audition. They notice me and then it all goes quiet apart from a few whispers but I can't make out what they are saying. I can't show them I'm nervous or they won't take me or this audition seriously and I don't want to let Roxy down because I am doing this for her. I finally made it to the table where I will be sitting which felt like it was miles and miles away. I take my seat, for a few seconds I just look out at the crowd, I can feel my throat going dry and my hands are sweating but all I keep thinking about is how I can't afford to mess this up.

"Morning ladies." I hear myself say.

"Morning." they all reply in unison

"I'm Jake, I work with Roxy Red" I state and technically I am telling the truth, they don't need to know that I am an apprentice. "Now unfortunately Roxy can't be here today so she has asked me to stand in for her." I continued.

"So basically what I want to see is how you walk, pose and then walk back, like you would on a runway, ok. They all nodded in agreement. " Ok so everyone line up against the wall and we will get started." The models are all lined up against the wall, all looking so serious. They were all very attractive, they were all roughly about the same height which Roxy did tell me that it was important that they all be about the same height. I was looking for models to be strong, confident and could hold a pose, like I had seen in so many magazines growing up and the models in front of me had all these qualities but they weren't smiling, not a single one. I knew they were nervous but I thought at least a few of them would have smiled by now, even a nervous smile but nothing.

I was just about to speak when the door burst open behind me. I turned to look who was late. She was wearing a pair of jeans with a white t-shirt and a pair of white trainers, her hair was long, brown and curly. She was cute. "Sorry I'm late, my mum's car broke down on the way here." She said a little out of breath as she slid her bag over to where the other girls had put their bags and then made her way over to the wall to line up.

"It's fine, we have only just started. I state. "What's your name?" I ask.

"Ashley.. Ashley Mode." she replied, trying to compose herself. She smiles at me, I smile back then carry on with the audition as I remembered where I am and what I am doing here.

The whole audition process was so gruelling, I thought this was going to be fun and maybe if Roxy was here doing all this and I was just observing it would have been different but because I am here doing it all by myself, it takes all the fun out of it.

I was reading the models CV's, their names, age, nationality, their previous modelling experiences. Some of them had done so much modelling considering they had only been doing it for a couple of years. As they were auditioning I was putting a tick next to their name if they would go through or not.

Finally after what felt like all day but turned out only to be two hours later all the girls had walked, posed and walked back in front of me and now they were just waiting for the results. This was going to be difficult as I had no idea who I was going to pick. I let them all have a 15 minute break but really I just wanted to see them all relax a little. They all went off in their groups of friends, chatting about fashion and the latest gossip that was going around. One girl was showing a funny video to her friends on her phone.

I'm standing near the window, I'm just about to text Roxy when I hear a voice a few metres away from me "she is so fat, he better not have her as one of his models and not me." I put my phone away and walk closer to hear what else this voice has got to say. "I mean, come on, she is so fat."

"She looks like a pig" one of the other girls joined in. They all started laughing.

I didn't think any of the girls were overweight. I looked over to see who they were talking about and there was Ashley sitting on the floor reading a book. She had no idea what had been said about her as she was too far away but I heard everything and what they were saying was enough for me to make the decision that none of them would be in the show.

"What are you reading?" I asked as I sat next to her on the floor.

She looked up at me, her dark blue eyes were the first thing I noticed, they were amazing. "oh, it's a love story, it's about a woman who is promised to one man but she is in love with another man, I know it's a cliche" she jokes.

"Sometimes cliche is a good thing."

"I agree, I love reading stories about love and romance and couples finding a way to be with one another even if they have to go through adversities to get there."

"Wow, I'm impressed."

"What did you think? All models are all airheads and can't read a book."

"No, not at all but I am impressed by it."

"Well thank you." she blushes. "So have you made a decision?" she asks.

"I think so," I replied coyly.

"And did I make the cut?"

"You will have to wait and see," I replied as I got to my feet. She smiled and I walked away.

I stood in front of the table where I had been sitting for the past few hours. I coughed to get their attention but a few of them didn't hear me and were still speaking so I coughed again, a little louder and eventually they stopped talking.

"Right, well firstly I want to thank each and everyone of you for coming to this audition today. It has been very eye opening to say the least" I didn't want to tell them that I was so glad that this was over. "but we are only looking for 10 models for this particular show so if I call your name please make your way over to that wall." I point over to the wall so they know where to stand.

"First up, Maria Polo". I see Maria get up with a huge smile on her face, she stands against the wall looking like she has just won the lottery.

"Next is Natalie Fox… Ruby Marcez…Jennifer Matic…Toni Native…Alice Mooney…Louise Black…Michelle Charge…Cindy Tork and finally Ashley Mode." I see Ashley's face as she hears her own name being called out, she is so surprised and happy at the same time.

"Everyone else, sorry and thank you for coming down." I did feel bad but it's not like I could put them all in the show. Roxy only wanted 10 models and unfortunately some people weren't going to make it.

As the models were all leaving with their disappointed faces I did overhear what the model who called Ashley "fat" said to her friend. She turned to her friend and said " I didn't want to be in this show anyway, I don't even know why I auditioned" and the friend agreed "yeah same." and they both walked out of the door and out of my life forever and I hope I never have the misfortune of meeting them ever again. I just laughed as I watched them walk away.

Chapter 9

Over the next few weeks I was so busy with the upcoming fashion show, early mornings, late nights. We skipped so many meals and when we did remember to eat, it was always a takeout at three in the morning from the local chinese restaurant down the street. Apparently it was always like this before a fashion show, so much to do and not enough time to do it in.

I saw Ashley a few times over the next couple of weeks, we would exchange a quick "hey" but that would be about it. We both had to be professional and I knew how important this opportunity was for her and I didn't want to ruin it for her.

Roxy was busy with the show but she always had time to hear my input about the collection so I was learning on the job. It was my opinion and she didn't have to listen to it and sometimes she didn't, which was fine but when she would, it felt nice to know that I had a part to play in the show.

It was the night of the show and I was so excited. To know that in a few hours I would be watching the show that we have been planning for the past 2 months. Everything had to be perfect, we had sorted and gone through everything twice to make sure that we haven't missed anything. Only the best guests would attend, what food the caterers would serve and when, the music, the lights, make sure that all the models would get there in time, to get them in hair and make up. I was on the phone the whole day, calling people of all industries asking if they were still attending, I only got through to either a PA or an agent but they did assure me that everyone who I called would be going and all I had to do was hope that they did so I was a little nervous because I can only imagine if no one turned up and Roxy looks like a laughing stock at her own fashion show and it's all my fault. She would probably kick me off the apprenticeship and then I would have to move back home and I couldn't allow that to happen. I have tasted this world and I am not going back to what my life was like.

The fashion show was taking place right here in the studio, it was Roxy's idea. Backstage where all the models were getting ready is where we would usually get together every morning and brainstorm new ideas about new collections. The runway itself managed to fit in the space where all of our tables once stood, compared to what it looked like a few hours before. The whole office had a total makeover. The lights had changed different colour which made a massive difference on its own, not to mentioned the fake walls that were up, the T.V screen that were showing clips of models over the years that Roxy had worked with even the runway itself, it was way bigger than I thought it was going to be, black and shiny.

The guests were arriving in their droves by half 7, the place was really starting to fill up. People from all forms of the entertainment industry was here, I saw models, actors, singers, even a pro basketball player came, I don't really remember his name but I knew who he was because he had his wife with him and I had seen her face in the fashion magazines before, she has got her own clothing line and whenever she can go to another designers show, she will be there. People were turning up who I definitely didn't know but they had a huge entourage of people with them so they had to be a big deal, maybe rappers, I'm not really that into rap music so it could be.

Whilst Roxy was mingling with her guests I went to see how everything was going backstage when I bumped into Ashley. Her brown hair was now straight and tied up in a tight, high ponytail, I almost didn't recognize her with makeup on but she still looked amazing. She was wearing an olive green off the shoulder dress, which really complemented her lightly tanned skin tone.

"Sorry…hey" I smiled when I recognized it was her.

"Hi" she smiled back.

"Are you nervous about going out there and all eyes being on you?" I asked flirtatiously.

"A little but I'll be fine" she replied calmly. No hesitation with her answer. I believed her when she said it.

"Well I will be watching you." as soon as I said it I knew how it sounded but it was too late to take it back so I had to think of something quick to say "I mean I won't be watching you" I can feel my cheeks get redder by the second "I mean I will be watching you but not just you, I will be watching the whole show." I feel like I may have just saved myself, only by the skin of my teeth.

"I know what you meant," she laughed. "I better go, I have to find my shoes to wear."

"I will see you after the show."

"Yeah, I'd like that." she smiled then walked off.

As she left, another model caught up to her and they started laughing together. She had the most amazing smile I had ever seen, she looked so beautiful. My thoughts were abruptly interrupted when I heard someone shouting, a woman shouting, a woman who I had never seen before.

"All I want to do is talk to Roxy!" she yelled at the security guard. Roxy hired two of them for the door for not just her protection but everyone's as there were some high profile people in this place and she didn't want anyone to just walk in.

"Miss Red is busy right now." the security guard replied back.

"I bet she is!" she shouted again. She tried to push her way past the guards but it was no good, he was at least three times her size and it was all muscle so no one was getting past him and there were two of them so even if by some miracle she managed to get past one, there was still the other one to consider.

Just then she sees Roxy walk past. Roxy is so busy laughing and enjoying a glass of champagne that at first she doesn't really notice that someone is shouting her name. "Roxy!.. Roxy!!!" The mystery woman tried to get her attention, she is still trying to fight her way out of the grasp of the security guard but it's no good, she keeps screaming her name. "Roxy!!!.... Roxy!!!.... ROXY!!!" and on that last scream Roxy finally turns around. As soon as Roxy and this mysterious woman make eye contact, Roxy's face changes, like all the colour drained from her face and she is frozen for a few seconds.

By the look on her face she knows exactly who this woman is but within a split second it's like she remembers where she is, she pulls a confused look on her face. "I'm sorry and you are?"

"YOU KNOW EXACTLY WHO I AM, BITCH!" She yelled at Roxy, not breaking eye contact with her.

"I'm sorry, I will not be spoken to like that on the day of my fashion show, security please throw this person outside." she walks away, carries on talking to her friends and makes her way back to the party and grabs another glass of champagne.

"ROXY, YOU WON'T GET AWAY WITH THIS!!!" she yells as she is being dragged away by security. Now I have about a million questions running through my head, who was that woman? What did she want? And more importantly what won't Roxy get away with? Roxy watched the woman being dragged away until she was no longer in her view. She ignored the people around her until the mystery woman was out of view and then she carried on with the conversation like nothing had happened

All I kept thinking about was Roxy's face when she first saw that woman, she knew who she was but how?

Now it was time for the fashion show, which even though it was my first fashion show I had attended, it was incredible. The outfits looked amazing, the models looked absolutely flawless, they walked with an attitude. When it was Ashley's turn to strut the runway, she was amazing. She owned the runway, like she had been doing it for years, the nerves if she had any didn't show.

Everyone was complimenting her on how beautiful she was, she responded so graciously. She had no idea how beautiful she was which made her even more perfect. She did not gloat when someone gave her a compliment or had an attitude, not like some of the other models, she was different.

I went backstage to talk to Ashley, she was sitting at a vanity table, wiping off the lipstick off her face. "Hey," she smiled at me through the mirror.

"Hi." I took the spare seat next to her.

"Thanks, I did ok." She was being modest.

There were a few moments of awkward silence between us, she looked at me, I instantly looked at the floor, I could feel my face going red. I thought that if I don't ask her for her number now then I never would. After three I'm going to ask her 1…2… but before I spoke she began to talk so we both interrupted one another.

"Sorry you go first." I apologised.

"No you go" she stared at me for a few seconds with a smile.

Here it goes, the worst thing she could say was no but I still didn't want to hear it so I took a deep breath and just hoped for the best.

"Do you want to go out sometime?" That question hung in the air for what felt like hours before she answered. I was calm on the outside but inside my heart was beating so fast. I have never done this before.

"Sure, when" she answered.

"Whenever you're free" I was too busy focusing on what she had just said that I didn't hear what she said next. I realised I haven't paid attention. "I'm sorry, what did you say?" I could feel my cheeks get more red than they were before.

"Do you have your phone with you?" she said with a laugh, she knew that I had spaced out for a minute and she found it funny.

"Sure, here it is" I hand over my phone, she presses the screen a few times.

"Here." She gives me my phone back. I look at the phone, she has put her number in my phone.

"Text me when you want to meet up." she says as she gets out of her chair and leaves.

"I will, I definitely will." I say with a smile.

Chapter 10

Over the next few weeks I spent most of the time with Ashley, now that all the chaos from the fashion show was finally over, we had time to get to know one another.

Even Roxy told me to get to know her. We were in the car the morning after the fashion show, on our way to the studio. I was tired but happy as I had been texting Ashley all night. I think I only had about two hours sleep but it was worth it.

"What are you so happy about?" I hear as I am smiling back at my phone after reading Ashleys latest text.

"Just so happy that the fashion show was a success but I am glad it's over." I didn't lie. I was happy about the fashion show and how it went but there was more than just that.

"So this has nothing to do with that model that I saw you talking with after the show yesterday."

I could feel my face blush.

" I know it's none of my business but you should spend a bit of time together, she seems really nice and let's face it you've earned some time off."

I thought about it for a few seconds whilst Roxy was looking through her brown handbag that was resting on her lap. "Here, take this." She hands me her credit card.

"I can't" I was so shocked that she just gave me her credit card.

"Yes you can, spend the day together, do whatever you like." she insisted.

"You sure you wont need me at the studio." I asked but I knew the answer.

Who needs the apprenticeship there when there are plenty of people around whose job it is to cope under the pressure that comes from working at a fashion house.

"I think the house of red will cope without you for a day" she said sarcastically. I smile.

I immediately texted Ashley.

Hey, got the day off, do you want to do something? X. I text her. I read the message I was debating with myself whether or not to put a kiss on the end but before I had a chance to delete it, the message was sent. As soon as I sent it it felt like I was waiting for days for a reply. Roxy was talking next to me but I wasn't really listening. I was looking out the window, the sky was grey, it was slightly raining but I didn't care. Then my phone vibrated.

Sounds good x

There it was, a kiss. Now I'm nervous.

We met up at a cafe which made sense as we were both hungry. As soon as I saw her, all I wanted to do was ask about the last text. Why did she put a kiss at the end, was it because I did and she was just being nice, did she put the kiss on the text to everyone and to her it meant nothing or did it mean something else completely. She looked stunning, wearing a pair of ripped jeans, a plain white t-shirt with a leather jacket over it, a pair of trainers and her hair was in a ponytail. She always looked amazing but even when she wasn't trying to, she still looked like she just came off a photoshoot.

She hugged me and I hugged her back, she smelt of coconuts.
"Hey, how are you?" she asked as she let go of me.
"Yeah I'm good, thanks, you?"
"Yeah I'm good, are we going in or what because I am starving" she said holding her stomach.
We went in and sat down, both of us were examining the menu to see what looked good but to me everything sounded delicious as I had missed breakfast. After a couple of minutes a waitress came over to take our order. Ashley ordered the poached eggs on toast and I ordered a stack of pancakes with syrup.

We engaged in conversation while we waited for our food to arrive. She told me stories from her childhood. When she was seven she did her first photoshoot, it was for a children's clothing line. Her mum signed her up for it just to earn a little extra money but she actually enjoyed it and that was where it all started for her and she has never looked back. When she was eleven she did her first ever advert, it was for chocolate cereal, she told me that they had to do so many takes of her eating the same cereal that by the end of it she hated the cereal and still can't eat it to this day.

When the food came over, we were deep in conversation. She was telling me about her mum and how close they are, how her mum had to sacrifice a lot to get her to auditions, callbacks and photoshoots. We were eating when I noticed that she had a little bit of egg on face, just beside her lip. She was talking but all I could do was focus on the egg. I let out a little giggle.

"What's so funny?" She looked confused but smiling.

"I'm sorry, it's just you have a little egg on your face." I explained.

She uses her finger to wipe her face but she wipes the wrong side.

"Did I get it?"

"No, here let me get it for you." I lean over to brush the egg off her face with my thumb, her skin is so soft. She looks at me, her eyes are inches away from mine, any closer and our noses would be touching.

"Is it all gone?" she asks as we are still staring at each other.

"All gone."

"Thanks" she breaks eye contact and looks back at her food.

I suddenly get nervous and look at my food too.

"So what do you fancy doing today?" I ask, my attempt at changing the subject.

"Ermm I don't know, whatever you want, I'm free the whole day".

"Do you like bowling?" I suggest.

"Love it but I haven't in years, my mum used to take me all the time but then my dad died and she had to go back to work." She took a sip of her coffee.

"I'm sorry, I had no idea about your dad."

"It's ok, it was a few years ago now, we knew it was coming so at least I got to say goodbye, not many people get that so for that I am grateful."

I smile at her, she has been through a lot but to see such a horrible experience in such a positive way, really says a lot about her. "So what about you?"

"What about me?"

"Well I'm assuming you have parents and weren't made in a laboratory somewhere, do you speak to them?"

This was the question I was dreading she would ask me. I wanted to tell her the truth not because she had just told me something personal but because I just didn't right now so I just spoke about my mum.

"Well my mum died a few years ago, brain tumour, one minute she was fine, next minute she was told she had six months to live, I still think about her everyday. She was the one who got me into fashion and designing. She would always ask for my opinion on an outfit when I was little, when she got invited to go somewhere, she was an a amazing woman"

"She sounds so cool"

"She really was" I often think about how cool my mum actually was and it always makes me smile.

After we finished our food we found a taxi to take us bowling. We talked in the taxi. She told me the time when she was eleven she was climbing in a tree, fell and broke her arm "I thought it was cool to have my arm in a cast for a few weeks." The way she spoke about her childhood was always positive, even when she speaks about her dad, it's always about the memories she has of him.

She has no siblings, a few good friends at school, she was a popular girl at school, even more so when people found out she was a model.

She threw a strike on her first go, I was amazed. I wasn't expecting that at all. "and that is how you do it." she said confidently as she made her way back so I could have my go.

"Just to let you know I'm not good at this game." I shyly tell her.

"That's ok." She reassures me.

I bowl with an orange ball and afterwards there isn't a single pin standing. I look back at her, "I'm great at this game."

"Sounds like we need to make this more interesting"

"I agree." I say as I walk over to sit next to her.

"How about the loser has to buy dinner."

"Deal"

"Deal." we shook on it, her hands were so soft.

We carried on playing, the game was so close. She got a strike on her last bowl, she looked so happy. She turned to me, walking back confidently and said to me "you're up."

I smiled, I got up, and picked up a red ball this time. All I kept thinking about was that I need to get a strike now to win the game, focusing on the pins in front of me. I bowled, I watched the ball roll the whole way down the lane, it took out nine of the ten pins, the tenth one wobbled but remained standing. "Maybe next time." I hear from behind me.

"Maybe"

"So where are you taking me for dinner."

We sat in a small restaurant, not too far from the bowling alley. I didn't see the name, I just noticed the tables and chairs as I looked in the window so I thought it would be a good place to eat in. We sat down and instantly a waiter came over to take our orders. Ashley ordered a carbonara and I had something called 'the house burger' which was just a beef burger with extra cheese but it was nice anyway.

Over the next few hours we just sat there and talked, we spoke about everything and anything. We talked about trivial topics like movies,

Ashley liked horror movies which I was never a fan of, I remember being when I was about 6/7 and my brothers managed to get a horror movie from somewhere and convinced me to watch it and I couldn't go to sleep for weeks after. "I like Comedy films, anything that makes me laugh."

We spoke about books and music and then we talked about more in depth topics like our life long goals and what we really want to achieve in life. We were just leaving the restaurant when I had a great idea.

"Do you want to come to the studio with me?" I ask, hoping she would say yes.

"I would love to, are you sure I'm allowed too?" she asked curiously.

I thought about it for a few seconds and maybe I wasn't allowed to bring people to the studio but then I thought about how no one would be there and it's not like we were going to steal anything or wreck the place so it should be fine.

"Yeah, it should be fine"

We get to the studio all the lights are off but Roxy's office light is still on, she must be working late or she has just lost track of time. "Would you mind just waiting here?" I whisper to Ashley in case Roxy hears me.

"Sure." Ashley is waiting at the table and is admiring all the sketches.

I creep forward to her office. I can hear Roxy's voice but I can't hear another person talking back to her. I peek round the door and I can't see her, her chair is facing the other way but I know she is there as I can see her tanned legs on the desk wearing her black stilettos. I am just about to walk in when I hear the next part of the conversation. " Yeah, he's so stupid, as if a model would ever go out with him." Is she talking about me? But why? I haven't done anything to her, no she must be talking about someone else, maybe an ex boyfriend or one of her friends. "I don't know, maybe she feels sorry for him" she carries on. "Or maybe she is just going out with him just to see if she can get more modelling jobs, I've done that before and more just to secure a modelling job" she starts to laugh. "Well he can go on all the dates he wants with her because I have got what I need from him, his designs which are safely locked away in my desk and Jake doesn't know where they are and that's all that matters." she starts to laugh again. She is talking about me, she was just using me for my designs, she was never interested in helping me at all, all she wanted was my designs and for her to take the credit for my work.

I stood there for a few seconds, thinking about what I had just heard when she turned around and she made eye contact with me. Her smile went instantly and her eyes went wide but then she tried to act like nothing was wrong. "G, I better go, I will call you tomorrow, bye." She put both of her legs off the table and back on the floor, she put the phone down slowly. "Jake, what are you doing here?" she asked nonchalantly.

I had to think about my answer as even though what I just heard, I didn't want Ashley to get in trouble. "I came back after my date to see if there was anything I could do and I saw the light on so.."

"So how was your date?" she asked with a fake smile, hoping that would move the conversation and we would talk about my date but I wasn't going to let her get away with it, not after what I just heard.

"Fine, I just thought I would come back to see if you needed my help with anything."

"Well as you can see everyone has gone home for the night so you might as well do the same." She interrupted me.

I stared at her for a few seconds before saying anything else, she had her perfect manicured hands clasped together on her desk.

"Who was that on the phone?" I asked. I know that I had no reason to know who she was talking to but when she is talking about me then I feel like I deserve to know who she was talking too.

"Oh that…that was no one." she stuttered.

"So you just picked up the phone and started talking…to no one." I didn't break eye contact with her. I felt a little nervous but I wanted to know.

"If you must know I was talking to my sister, Gina but I call her G for short, happy?" she asks with a slight annoyance in her voice.

"Why were you talking about me?" I asked her. I could feel myself getting angry by just looking at her.

"Yeah I was." she admitted it, like it was nothing. Like I had just asked her for the time or something, no emotion on her face.

"Why?" I am really confused how she could just turn like that. One minute she doesn't want to tell me who she is talking to and the next she is telling me not only who she was talking to but what she was talking about.

"Hasn't it dawned on you yet?" she said in her patronising voice. Talking to me like I'm a child, I hate it when people talk to me in this tone of voice. My brothers used to talk to me like this all the time.

"What."

"I no longer need you here. I have your designs and they will be great for MY new collection." She took a sip of coffee whilst looking at me over the cup.

"You can't do that, they are my designs!" I shout.

"Jake , you seriously have got so much to learn about this business. Number one rule in this industry, people in this business only lookout for themselves."

"Well I will tell everyone you stole them from me." I threatened her.

"And who do you think people are going to believe, me a very successful fashion designer who has her own company or you, a no one who is still searching for their fathers approval and we both know you will never get that."

The anger is burning inside of me, how could I have been so stupid, she only wanted my designs, she had no intentions of helping me at all.

"Where are my designs?" I asked her but I knew where they were but I wanted to know if she would tell me.

"They are safe and ready for me to show my team in a few days." She grinned at me. "So why don't you get out of my office, go back to the house, pack your stuff and get out of MY house, if you don't then I have no problem calling the police."

I leave without saying another word to her. I walk a few steps then I see Ashley who I forgot was here at all, standing just outside the door.

"Hey, you alright?" she asks me quietly as we walk to the main door.

"Not really, I'm homeless and out of a job, not the best way to end our date" we both laughed slightly.

"You could always stay at mine on the sofa, I'm sure my mum won't mind."

"Thanks"

We got into a taxi and went to the house to pack my stuff up, we were a few minutes away when Ashley held on to my hand and looked at me. I looked at her back. "She was wrong, you know?"

"Who was?" I was confused.

"Roxy."

"What do you mean? I didn't realise that she had heard any of the conversation.

"I didn't go on this date because I felt sorry for you or to get more modelling jobs. I genuinely like you and even though the end of the date has been interesting, I've had a good day today."

"Me too." I agree. "Apart from the last bit."

We both smiled.

Ellen, Ashley's mother was just about to leave for her night shift at work when we got there. She worked night shifts as a nurse which was only a 5 minute walk from where they lived. She didn't seem to mind me staying after Ashley explained all that had happened.

"That's awful." she said whilst eating some toast that Ashley made for her. "Well of course you can stay here until you find somewhere else, we can't have you roaming the streets, it's not safe."

"Thank you so much, I really do appreciate it." I said graciously. She didn't have to, she doesn't owe me anything and yet she is still allowing me to stay in her home.

She headed off to work while I made a bed for myself with the blankets and pillows Ellen gave me. The sofa was very comfortable which was surprising. I was so tired that all I remember was saying goodnight to Ashley as she went upstairs to bed and that was it until morning.

Chapter 11

The next morning I woke up to Ashley and her mum talking in the kitchen. I looked out the window but I couldn't see the sun or any daylight, it still looked like it was nighttime. I picked up my phone that was on the table in front of me, it read 7.12am. Ellen must be back from her nightshift. I walk into the kitchen, they are both eating and talking, Ashley notices me first. "Hey, did you sleep alright?" She looks adorable in her pink fluffy pyjamas, her hair is a little messy. She doesn't look like she has been awake long.

"Yeah, fine thanks." I reply as I rub my eyes.

"Good, do you want any breakfast?"

"Just a coffee please"

"Sure." Ashley gets up to make me a coffee. I sit on one of the other chairs.

Ellen smiles at me. I smile back.

"Are you sure you don't want anything to eat?" Ellen asks before taking a sip of her coffee but I assure her I am fine.

"Ok, well it was lovely meeting you again." She gets up to take her cup to the sink.

"Nice to meet you too and thanks again for letting me stay here."

"You're welcome." She takes one last gulp of her coffee before putting the cup in the sink. "Right, I'm off to bed for a few hours, make sure you lock the door when you go out as I won't be awake when you leave." she says to Ashley.

"I will." She answers her as she is stirring my coffee. Ellen kisses Ashley on the cheek then goes up stairs.

"Are you going out?" I ask her as she comes back over to the table.

"Yeah, I got a waitress job at a private event this afternoon." she informs me.

"Oh I didn't know you did that." I didn't mean to sound surprised, I just wasn't expecting her to say something like that.

"Yeah I do it sometimes to help my mum out with the bills, it's not fair that she is the only one who has to work." she explains. "It's my mum's friend who owns the catering company so every now and then I just pick up events that I can do, this way I can still earn money and keep doing my modelling."

"Wow, I think it's great you help out so much, you seem like you and your mum have such a close bond." I envy her in some way.

I never got to have a close bond like that with my mum in my teen years.

"After everything we have been through over the last few years we are closer than ever and even though she does annoy me most of the time, I don't know what I would do without her." She takes a sip of her coffee. "So what is the plan?" she asks changing the subject.

"Well as lovely and comfortable as your sofa is, I can't stay on it forever. I can't go back home and Roxy has my designs so I haven't a clue what I am going to do.

"Well why don't you just stay here until we can think of a plan?"

"Would you mum allow me to stay here? I mean it's one thing spending one night here but more than that, shouldn't we ask her first." I don't want Ellen to think that I am just looking for somewhere to stay for free.

"We were talking about it when you were asleep and she said that you are more than welcome to stay here until you sort yourself out."

"Really." I feel relieved as I did think that I would be sleeping on a park bench tonight but thanks to Ellen and Ashley kind hospitality that won't be happening.

Ashley goes upstairs to get ready for her job later. I wash up the pots and tidy the kitchen plates, it's the least I can do for them both. After I wash up I go into the living room and put the TV on, they don't have many channels to choose from but I'm not really watching it. Ashley comes downstairs and into the living room wearing a white blouse and a pair of black trousers, her hair is now brushed and in a ponytail. "Have you seen my phone?" she asks as she enters the room and starts looking under magazines on the coffee table but before I could answer her she had already found it.

She checks her phone to check the time. "Right, I'm off, I will only be a few hours, are you going to be ok on your own for a while?" she asks whilst putting on her coat.

"Yeah I will be fine." I assured her. I watched her leave and walk down the street to the bus stop.

I make myself comfortable on the sofa and search through the channels trying to find something to watch, try to take my mind off everything that is going on but nothing good is on so I just put on anything. I put on a reality show but I know it's not all real but I keep watching.

About an hour goes by, the reality show is getting interesting. Matt, one of the main guys, was talking to another girl in this nightclub and his girlfriend had just found out. They were in the middle of an argument when my phone rang. I picked it up. It was Ashley.

"Hello."

"Hey" she is speaking really quietly "you need to get down here right now."

"Is everything ok? Why are you talking so quietly?" I was concerned.

"I'm not meant to be on my phone but I needed to call you so I'm currently in the bathroom of this mansion so I could call you." she explains but I am still confused.

"Why did you need to call me?" I am even more confused.

"Do you know who Clive Million is?" she asks.

"Of course I do"

Clive Million is a world famous bachelor, he is the only son to Martha and Malcome Million, who were big country singers back in the day but he keeps himself relevant by dating the latest models and singers who are only dating him because they think that it would be good for their career but it never lasts long. He got married last year to a model but the marriage only lasted 3 months.

"Well I am at his birthday party right now."

"Ok" I replied not knowing where this conversation was going. "So what has that got to do with me"

"Well because I have just overheard him talking to one of his friends about investing in something new and different."

"Ok… I'm still not following." I am even more confused than before.

"Come on Jake, do you want me to spell it out for you." she almost shouts down the phone.

"I think you're going to have to." I calmly replied back.

"He could invest in your fashion line, give you the capital to get your designs made and get your collection out there for the world to see." I thought about it for a few seconds. Having someone like Clive Million behind the collection would be amazing and with his contacts, it would be a huge help in getting my designs out there.

"Send me the address"

I suddenly felt excited, my mind was rushing with the thought of this meeting going well and him loving my designs.

I got dressed and made my way down to where the event was being held. The mansion that the taxi drove me to was so big, it was secluded by trees, the house was a beige colour with a water fountain in the front of it. I could hear a piano playing faintly in the background. I knocked on the door and waited but no one answered so I knocked again but still there was no answer. I didn't want to just open the door but I knew that someone was in because it wasn't just the music I could hear but I could hear people talking very faintly but I could hear them nonetheless so I opened the door and to my surprise the door opened. "Hello." I spoke softly as I entered but I couldn't hear much but the piano and the voices which were a little louder now. I couldn't take my eyes off the white marble staircase that was in front of me, it was amazing to see something so grand like that in someone's house.

I saw Ashley walking down the corridor, she was holding a black jacket and she was walking very fast towards me. "Here quick put this on" she demands me and helps me put the jacket on. "I stole it from where they keep the uniforms." She tells me. The black jacket actually fits well and makes my current outfit more stylish. I didn't know what the dress code for this event was and as I wasn't invited I didn't want to stand out too much as I didn't want to draw attention to myself so I went with a white t-shirt, smart black trousers and a pair of black shoes so the jacket looks like I made the decision to wear it myself.

"So where is he?" I ask as she takes the jacket that I was wearing and shoves it into a nearby empty plant pot.

"He is out there." she replies back as she is folding back the lapels on my jacket, trying to make me look as smart as possible so no one knows that I am not supposed to be here.

She guided me to the garden where everyone was, waiters were walking around offering appetisers to the guests, the guests were talking, drinking champagne. I could hear laughing but I couldn't see where it was coming from. The pool looked so clean but no one was in the water, people were just walking around it. I saw a woman playing the piano which I heard the moment I arrived.

I was looking around at everyone, taking it all in, the whole scene when I saw him. Mr Clive Million. He was about 6ft tall, silver hair, which matched his short beard, he was tanned but not too much. He was wearing a pair of jeans and a soft red turtleneck. He was standing just a few metres away from me. He was talking to a few people. I didn't want to go over and disturb him, I was just about to turn around when I made eye contact with Ashley, she looked at me and just by her look I knew what she would say if she could speak to me. "Go" she mouthed to me. I closed my eyes, took a deep breath and walked over to him.

"Excuse me. Mr Million." I tap him on the shoulder.

He turns around and looks at me with his stunning blue eyes. He takes a sip of his champagne and smiles. "Oh please, Mr Million was my father, call me Clive."

I felt less worried now as I was now speaking to him, the nerves just left and I carried on the conversation. "Well Clive, I just came over to introduce myself. I'm Jake Silver."

"Nice to meet you Jake" he shakes my hand.

"I was just wondering if I could have a moment of your time. I understand that this is your party and you are a very busy man but if I could talk to you about a business opportunity that I think you would be interested in."

Well I did it, I asked him now it's all up to him even if he is not interested at least I can say I gave it a try.

"Well I'm always on the lookout for new business ventures so let's go to my office and chat." he leads me back inside the house to go to his office. I smile at Ashley as we head back inside and she smiles back.

"Can I offer you a drink?" he says as he opens the door to his office

"No thanks." He makes his way over to his desk and sits down, behind him is a massive window where the party is still going on outside as I can see people walk past.

It wasn't a big office but it was big enough. For the size of this house I thought it was going to be this huge office with a massive fireplace, a huge desk and a lot of antiques in it but it wasn't. It was decorated very simple and minimalist, white walls, a few pieces of artwork, 2 black leather sofas, a grey carpet and a bookcase on the other side of the room, full of books of all genres.

"Please have a seat." he offered me. I sat down after looking at his books.

"Thank you." I sat down.

"So, you said that you had a business opportunity for me, let's hear it." he said, crossing his arms.

I was telling him everything about what happened between me and Roxy and how that ended, I was just explaining the last conversation with Roxy I had when he interrupted.

"Let me guess, she stole your designs."

How did he know that? Were they somehow working together?

"Yes, how…how did you know that?" I stuttered nervously.

"Let's just say I am familiar with Roxy and we have unfinished business."

"Ok." I am intrigued. I was trying to figure out what he meant by that but I didn't want to pry into his business.

"From everything that you have told me, I really want to see your designs and possibly investing. So why don't I give you my card and call me tomorrow about setting up a meeting where I can see your designs, sound good?"

"That sounds amazing." Is this actually happening to me? I can't believe it.

We shake hands and we both make our way back to the party. He sees some friends and walks over to them and I look around to find Ashley.

I see Ashley walking back to the kitchen, I run over to her, tap her on the shoulder.

"He wants to set up a meeting." I say excitedly whilst showing her the card he gave me, we both hug and out of nowhere we share another kiss.

"Sorry" I apologise.

"Yeah we shouldn't have done that here, not very professional of me." Fortunately no one was around to see that because I didn't want her to get sacked.

"Yeah it wasn't" I agreed looking at the floor, slightly embarrassed.

"So what did he say?" she asked, trying to change the subject.

"I have to call him and set up a meeting."

"That's amazing."

"And he wants to discuss working with me."

"That's amazing." she repeats but still sounds excited for me.

"And he wants to see my designs."

"Thats am…wait what." her face changes suddenly, her smile has completely gone.

"What…what's wrong?"

"Roxy has your designs so how are you going to show him if you don't have them?"

I think about it for a few seconds, processing what she has just said.

"You're right." The excited feeling suddenly disappears and now all I can feel is anxiety.

"We need to come up with a plan to get your designs back." Ashley suggests.

"Ok and how do we do that?"

"Well firstly you are going to go back to mine and I will help you when I get back."

We hug and I leave to go back to her house to start thinking of a plan to get my designs back.

Chapter 12

The plan was simple: sneak into her office, get the folder from her desk and get out. I knew that she doesn't get into the office before 9 o'clock so she isn't the problem, the problem is Ester the receptionist at the main desk, she gets to work an hour before anyone else. No one really pays any attention to her but I noticed her my first day. I asked Roxy who it was and she just said "Oh I don't know, no one." she said almost like she couldn't bear to look at her.

Ester sat at her desk when we got there, she was on her computer typing away when Ashley walked in first, she was going to distract her whilst I went up the stairs to her office. "Hey, Ester right?" Ashley asked but she knew that.

"Yeah." Ester responded with a puzzled look on her face. I could see she was trying to workout in her brain where she knew Ashley from but couldn't remember. "Can I help you with something?"

"I'm glad you asked, I wonder if you can help me. I was here yesterday and I lost my purse so when I got home I called up here and Roxy said she put it behind the receptionist desk so could you have a look for me."

As soon as I saw Ester put her head down to have a look for this invisible purse I ran towards the door that leads to the stairs. I ran up the stairs which wasn't so bad. I would have taken the lift but Ester might have seen me as it was opposite to her desk so the stairs were my safest option without being seen.

Once I was in Roxy's office I dashed straight over to her desk, which I found out was locked. The only way to get in there was if I knew the combination to it, which I didn't. For a few seconds I just looked at it, trying to work out what the combination could be. I knew it was a four digit number but didn't know which four numbers it was or the order they went in so I tried 1234, 0000, 2023 (the current year) and then I thought about how most people set codes to an important date so I tried her birthday, february 23rd, 2302 and I heard the lock from inside move and the door open. I smiled to myself that I had outsmarted someone like Roxy but then I remembered why I was here and what I needed to get.

There it was, my folder just there, waiting for me to take it. I grab the folder and quickly lock the door. I stand up and smile whilst I look at my folder.

I can't believe I have got my folder back, I quickly go through it to make sure my designs are still here and they all are. I close it back up and head for the door. I touch the handle when I hear a voice coming from the other side. It's Roxy! I can't hear another voice so she must be on the phone. With my body filled with panic I hide behind the curtains behind the desk. I managed to get behind the curtains just before she walked through the door.

"I've got a million and one things to do today." she says down the phone. She sits down at her desk. I am just a few feet away from her and she has no idea that I am even here, nevermind that I have got my designs back and as long as I keep quiet and not make a noise then I should be fine. "Well I have got this meeting later on today to show them my new collection, I'm so excited." I can hear the excitement in her voice which makes the anger inside of me rise up.

She is still claiming that my designs are hers and she is still going to take the credit for them. "Can I call you back G, I have another call coming through but speak soon sis, love you." I peak at the side of the curtain, her back towards me. Roxy presses her screen to accept the other call and starts speaking. "Ricky, darling, how are you?" She speaks in that horrible posh accent that she puts on for people who are more famous, more rich, more powerful than her, it's all for show. "You are here now, no worries. I am just getting in the lift now and I will meet you downstairs." I hear her say as she gets up and practically runs to the door.

I wait a few seconds just to make sure she has gone and then I quickly walk to the door, folder still in hand. Hopefully Ashley has left or hidden somewhere because if Roxy sees her, the whole plan could be ruined if she recognizes her. I walk down the stairs as I know that I am never going to run into Roxy on the stairs as she would rather die than climb the stairs, even if it's just a few flights.

I reach the bottom, I slowly open the door that leads to the main reception. Ester is not at her desk and Roxy must have already met her guest and gone back in the lift so this would be a great opportunity to leave now. I walk out of the door quickly. I can feel my heart beating so fast, thinking that I am about to get caught by Ester or even worse Roxy. I get to the main door, open it and I can feel the wind from the outside hit my face and it feels like I can breathe again. I take a deep breath in and back out. I close my eyes and take another deep breath in and back out. I can feel my heart calming down when there is a hand on my left shoulder. I turn around in shock, dropping my folder on the gravel, only to see Ashley standing in front of me. "Are you ok? She asks.

"Yeah I'm fine." I reply back in between deep breaths.

"Come on, let's get out of here." she says as she picks up my folder from the floor.

We get back to Ashley's house and I immediately call Clive to arrange an appointment to see him. I was so nervous dialling the number but I managed to arrange the appointment without stuttering ,sounding calm the entire time but all I wanted to do was scream from the excitement that I was feeling but there was a part of me that told me to be professional. We arranged an appointment for 10 o'clock the next morning at his office. I was excited and nervous at the same time that I barely got any sleep. Would he like my designs? Are they good enough? Would he really want to invest? All these questions were circling my mind all night.

Chapter 13

The next morning I'm so nervous I don't eat anything. Ellen did offer me some toast but I kindly declined. I have been up most of the night looking over my designs, seeing if there is anything I could improve on but the more I stared at them, the more I kept questioning my own work. At least one thing was off my mind and that was that all my work was back with me. I did have a brief moment of panic when I thought to myself that Roxy would have taken some designs out and moved them somewhere else but when I looked through the folder, they were all here.

Ellen leaves for work and Ashley and I get ready for this meeting with Clive. Ashley wears a black jeans with cream heel ankle boots, a white t-shirt and a long beige coat with her hair down, she looks like she has just come off a photoshoot. She looks amazing. I went in a pair of light grey chinos, white button up shirt and a black jacket. I did think about a tie but I chose not to wear it in the end but as we were in the taxi I did think about it and how I wished I had put one on.

"Are you nervous?" Ashley asks me.

"A little."

"I can tell." she says smiling. "Because your leg has not stopped shaking since we got in this taxi." She laughs. I look down and my leg is shaking, I hadn't even noticed. I was too busy thinking about this meeting.

"Sorry." I apologise and try to calm my leg down.

"You're nervous, it's understandable."

A few minutes later we pulled up outside the building where Clive's office is. It was a tall building almost like a skyscraper, it looked like the whole building was made out of glass. Ashley opened the main door and we took the lift up to the 24th floor. The doors opened and there was a desk straight ahead of us with a young man sitting behind it.

"Hello, how can I help you?" he asked, sounding very pleasant.

"I have a meeting with Clive Million." I replied, trying to sound as pleasant as him.

He typed on his keyboard for a few seconds, "Jake Silver at 10 o'clock" he said with a smile.

"That's right."

"Well I will let Mr Million know that you're here but in the meantime please take a seat and he will be with you shortly." He showed us to a leather sofa and we both sat down.

"Do you want me to come in the room with you?" Ashley asks politely.

"If you don't mind, I need to do this by myself." I feel so bad not letting her join me in this meeting as it was her who got me to meet with him in the first place and she has stuck by me through everything since being kicked out by Roxy.

"No, it's fine. I get it. Don't worry, this is your thing." she says. A part of me wants her to come to the meeting with me but there is another part of me that wants to do this by myself, to prove to everyone but most importantly to prove to myself that I can do it. I hold her hand, I am just about to speak when I hear a voice say my name.

"Jake Silver." the personal assistant says. "Clive is ready for you."

I follow him into the double doors. This office was so much different from his office at home. For one thing the view was different, you could see most of London from this view out of the floor to ceiling windows, the marble floor which was so clean it was almost like looking into a mirror every time I looked down at it. His desk was different from the other one, a glass table which I didn't like but I didn't tell him that.

"Jake, how are you?" Clive asks as soon as he sees me. The doors close behind me.

"I'm very well thank you and you?" I ask. My mother always told me that from when I was a child, that if someone asks you how you are, you tell them but then you ask how they are, it's a small gesture but it means a lot.

"I'm very well thank you, please have a seat, drink?" he asks.

"No thanks, a little too early for me." I regret it as soon as I say it. Maybe he won't even want to have this meeting with me, he probably thinks I am so boring because I am not having a drink.

"Yeah." he looks down at his watch. "Maybe you're right, it is a little early."

I watch him as he walks back over to his desk. He is wearing a dark blue suit, looking very sharp and dapper, it looks like the suit is made for him personally, like he's had it especially tailored for him which doesn't surprise me at all.

"So can I have a look at your designs?" he asks, as he takes a seat behind his desk.

I completely forgot that I was even holding the folder with my designs in it as I was too focused on his office and how different it was to his home office. "Sorry…sure… here you go." I passed the folder to him.

He takes the folder and sits back in his chair and flicks through it. He doesn't say anything, he just turns the page, stares at the design for a few seconds, then flips over to the next. I just stay completely silent, not making a sound. What is going through his mind as he looks at my designs? Is he thinking about changing anything? Does he even like the designs? Does he… My thoughts get interrupted when I see him look up, I smile nervously.

"You designed all of these?" He asks, showing no emotion on his face.

"Yes I did, why is there something wrong?" I am now nervous, why would he ask that. Does he think I am stealing another designer's work?

"No, nothing is wrong." He carries on looking through the designs. "These are really amazing." he says as he looks back down at them. I feel instant relief and all the worries that I have been carrying around with me all day like a heavy brick has now completely gone.

"I'm glad you like them." I say with relief.

"No, I don't like them… I love them." he continues "do you know what I see when I look at these designs?" he asks but I don't know what he's talking about.

"Erm.. clothes." I nervously reply.

"No, I see determination, someone who has put a lot of time and effort into these designs." He gets up and walks around to me. "Tell me Jake, why do you want to do this?"

"Do you mean to design clothes?"

"Yeah, why do you want to do it?"

I take a deep breath and think about it for a few seconds. "My father wanted me to take over the family business but I refused because I knew that if I did that and did what he wanted, I would forever be miserable and that thought terrified me more than anything else I have been through."

He walks back over to his side of the desk without saying another word. He looks at me as he sits down.

"You remind me of me." he finally spoke after a few seconds of silence.

"Thank you." I didn't know if I should have said that but it was too late.

"I take it that you know who my parents were?

"Yeah, sort of." which wasn't a lie. I knew who they were but not much.

"Well firstly my parents were amazing parents. When they were around, in my early years I would go on tour with them, we went all over the world but as I got older and needed to go to school, they would go without me, leaving me for months at a time." He picks up a photo frame from his desk and holds it. "I can't tell you how many birthdays and christmases I spent alone or with friends but when it was time for me to go to college my parents wanted me to go back on tour with them, neither of them went to college and it seemed to work out well for them so they didnt think college was a good fit for me but I knew that if I didn't go to college, the only thing I would be remembered for is being their son and nothing else, so I had a choice to make, go to college and make a name for myself or go on tour and forever live in their shadow."

"What did you decide to do?" I was intrigued by his story.

"I went to college and made a whole new life for myself." he states. "So what if every now and then someone refers to me as Malcome and Martha's son, it doesn't bother me. It would have been a lot worse for me if I had gone on tour with them and forever lived in their shadow."

I commend him for standing up to his parents and for doing what he did, it takes courage to stand up to anyone but especially your parents.

"Wow, it takes courage to do that, I know what it's like to stand up to your parents."

"So you are all on your own then?" he asks, putting the frame back on his desk.

"Pretty much."

"Well I want to invest in you, I think your designs are amazing." He says, flicking through the folder. "If we are going to do this when we are going to this properly and have a proper fashion show and I have some contacts in the fashion industry, models, buyers, photographers." I let him keep talking as I was too shocked to speak. I can't believe this is happening. "I have got just the person who I can ask to organise such an event." He picks up the phone. "Get me Selena Flores's number."

"Who is Selena Flores?" I was confused.

"Best event organiser in the business, known her for years. I want this event to happen in the next 12 weeks and I know it's not a lot of time but if anyone can do it she can, she's perfect."

"In 12 weeks, I gotta find a studio and a seamstress and…and." I could feel myself getting hot, my whole body was filling up with nerves again.

"Don't worry, I will take care of all of that." he says very calmly which makes me calm down a little. His phone rings and after a few rings he answers it. "Great, put her through." he says.

Clive is silent for a few seconds then he speaks. " Selena, how are you? I'm all good thank you for asking, so I need to ask you for a favour" he looks at me and smiles.

I can't believe this is happening.

Chapter 14

I met Selena Flores the day after I had my meeting with Clive, we met at a restaurant where she was planning another event. I went to meet her alone as Ashley had another event she was hired for.

Selena was a tall woman with long black hair, tanned skin and just a little make up, she was carrying around a folder sort of like the folder that I had my designs in but it was a different colour.

"Are you Jake?" she asked me.

"Yeah and you must be Selena."

"The one and only." she nearly shouts. A few of the people who are in the restaurant look over to see who was shouting but she doesn't seem embarrassed. "Right shall we have a seat and discuss this fashion show." We sit down at a nearby table and she opens her folder and she is already talking about colour schemes and what kind of different foods she wants me to have. I look in the folder that she has laid out on the table and I'm amazed at how much work she has already put into this as she has only known about it for the last 24 hours.

"Now this is just a rough sketch but this is how I think the runway should look, what do you think?" She showed me a bunch of sketches and they're amazing.

"Wow, that's incredible, how did you do that this fast?" I was astonished.

"I didn't draw it, David, my amazing sketch artist did. I told him what I wanted and he created this and I always trust his vision."

"Well, I love it." I inspect them further and he has drawn the whole room and he's not left anything out. The runway, the tables and chairs, the decor, he has even drawn a few guests to make the picture come to life. The colour scheme he drew the picture in was a white and blue combination and I thought the two colours worked so well together.

About an hour later and the table is full of sketches and other pieces of paper with lists of caterers that Selena would recommend we use, a list of fashion buyers and celebrity guests that Clive knew, a list of different photographers that Selena had used in the past for different events. "Whilst I've got you here, do you have any family I could put on the guest list?" Selena asks whilst writing something else down.
"Oh.. erm no, none of my family will be going."
"No one at all, parents, siblings, friends." she says, completely surprised. I bet she thought I was going to give her a long list of people to invite but the truth was that, it's not like I didn't want to invite my dad but I knew he would never come so it would be pointless asking him.
"Only Ashley but she will arrive with me." I utter.
"Ok then, do you mind if we leave it here as I have got another appointment to get too but we will talk more later and don't worry I have got everything sorted." she packs up her things and leaves.

That was the first and last time I ever sat down with Selena, for the next 12 weeks just went by so quickly. Everyday I was doing something different, Selena and I would talk on the phone almost everyday sorting out plans and finalising details about the event. It was incredible to see this whole event that merely weeks ago was just a sketch on a piece of paper but now it was coming together and into the real world.

I hadn't been to the studio where the fashion show would be taking place as I was too busy creating the collection that I was going to be showing. I had a whole team creating my collection. I was in awe of every single person on the team, their passion and ambition, their attention to detail was just amazing.

The night before the show, Ashley and I had decided to go and have a look and see it all, now it had all been done. The runway was built, the tables were fully decorated, the whole studio space looked so different from a few weeks ago when I came, there was only half a runway, there were a lot of construction workers who were still building, there was even a wall that was still showing the brick work. I did have a worry that it wouldn't be finished in time but Selena reassured me that in the next couple of weeks I wouldn't recognize the place and she was right, it looks so different.

"Wow, this looks better than what it did a few weeks ago." Ashley exclaimed when she saw the studio. She had not been to see it either, she was busy with work and she had a few modelling jobs that she took.

"I know it looks amazing." I agree, smiling as I look around. "Now follow me, I have got a surprise for you, close your eyes." I tell her and she does. With her eyes closed I guide her so she doesnt hurt herself, we walk a few metres and I stop her. "Wait here." I say. I came back a few moments later. "Ok ,now open." A mannequin stood before her, wearing a hot pink gown with spaghetti straps, she looked at it with amazement. "Wow, did you design that?" she asks in a quiet voice.

"Yeah, it's the final outfit of the collection." I admit.

"It's gorgeous." she steps nearer to it to admire it closer.

"I want to know if you would model it for me tomorrow in the show as the finale."

"What? You… you want me to model this masterpiece in your show." she stutters.

"Yeah, I've spoken to Selena about it and she thinks it's a great idea so what do you say?"

"I would be honoured to." We both smile at each other. "Can I try it on now?" she asks.

"Yeah , if you want to."

She takes the dress off the mannequin and rushes off with it over her arm, she goes behind a few cardboard boxes that havent been moved yet. "So have you thought of a name yet?" she asks me over the boxes.

"A name… for what?" I asked confusingly .

"For your brand, like what is your brand going to be called?" She explains.

"Oh I see, I was thinking about just calling it Jake Silver, keep it simple, that's what the best designers do, just have it as their own name."

"Fair enough, so I am now wearing a Jake Silver original." She walks out from behind the cardboard boxes, she looks breathtaking, like something I have never seen before.

"I guess you are." I smile at her.

She twirls for me so I can see what it looks like from all angles and it looks perfect, it fits her like a glove.

After she spends looking at herself for a few minutes in the mirror she goes back behind the boxes to take it off. I sit down at the edge of the runway just taking it all in.

Looking out at the empty room and all the things I have been through the last few months and how I wish my mum was here to celebrate with me. When she's finished Ashley comes and sits next to me.

"Are you ok?"

"Yeah, I'm just thinking about my mum and how she should be here, she would have loved all of this, the glitz and glamour. She would be my guest of honour and she would be cheering me on from the crowd." I smile as I think about her.

"If she could see you now, she would be so proud of you for not giving up on your dreams, especially after all you have been through to get here." Ashley grabs my hand. We stare at each other and then we share another kiss.

Chapter 15

It's the night of the show and even though the whole place looks stunning, I'm so nervous. The music is on, just loud enough for everyone to hear it, the champagne is flowing. There are so many guests, all dressed up in their best clothes, hair and make up done, wearing their finest jewellery. A few celebrities have even turned up. Clive arrived about 10 minutes after I did, with two models hanging from each arm, a typical entrance for him.

I went backstage to see how all the models were getting on, there was so much movement it was so difficult to focus on one thing. Some models were in chairs having their makeup done, some were getting sprayed with hairspray. I saw one model run around trying to find her pair of shoes that she was meant to be wearing. She was worried because she was the first model to be walking the runway and we were going to be starting soon.
"Where are they?" she asked in a panic as she ran by me but before I could help her she had already run off and she was too quick for me. Ashley was in her chair, applying her lipstick when I went over to see her.
"Hey."
"Hey." she greets me whilst still looking in the mirror. "How are you feeling?"
"I'm all good, better now that guests are starting to arrive." That was one of my biggest fears about tonight, that no one would turn up and

after all the hard work that has gone into tonight over the past few months would have been for nothing.

We talk for a little bit longer when Selena comes over to us both.

"Excuse me Jake, Clive wants to see you."

"Ok, thank you."

Selena walks off.

"I gotta go but I will see you just before you go on."

"Ok but you don't have to, I will be fine."

I walk off and head over to where Clive is standing, he is talking to a woman who looks familiar to me but I can't remember where I have seen her before.

"Clive, you wanted to see me."

"Yes Jake, I would like to introduce you to someone, this is Louise, my best friend's daughter, she is also an aspiring fashion designer."

With that last sentence still in the air I recognized who she was and where I recognized her from.

"You were that lady who called Roxy a bitch, a few months ago at her fashion show." I was shocked. Why was she here? Was she here for revenge?

"Yeah, not my finest moment." she says with a smile. She seems friendly enough.

"Well given the circumstances I think you had every right to call her that?" Clive said in a matter of fact way.

"I don't follow, what circumstances?" I asked curiously, there was clearly more to this story and I wanted to know what.

"Well there are a few things you don't know about Roxy." she began to explain. "Firstly she is close to bankruptcy, she may look like she has got all this money but in reality she has only got that money from taking out countless loans from the bank and other sources."

Is she really trying to tell me that Roxy Red, one of the most famous and successful designers in the world, is actually in debt?

"Secondly I used to work for her, she hired me as an apprentice and let me go after a few months as she only wanted my designs so she could steal them and pass them off as her own, she hasn't designed anything for years, she has constantly been doing this to people for years and the reason she picks on young people is that if anyone would say anything, accuse her of stealing, who is everyone going to believe, one of the worlds most successful designers or someone who nobody knows."

"Did you not tell anyone anyway?" I asked. I felt so sorry for her and if what she was saying was true then Roxy really is a bitch.

"I told my parents but as we didn't have proof, there really wasn't a lot they could do so when uncle Clive told me about the meeting that you had in his office and that you had been through a similar situation. I had to come and meet you. I know you had nothing to do with what happened to me. I hope you don't mind me coming tonight?" She looked a little nervous.

"Absolutely not and I'm sorry for what happened to you." I don't know why I apologised. I had no idea what Roxy was up to.

"It's ok, I know you had no idea what was going on so I don't blame you."

"So what are you going to do now?" I ask curiously.

"Start again, design a new collection and now I have got financial backing from uncle Clive here." she smiled at him. "I can host my own fashion show in just a couple of months and finally have my dream come true."

"And when you do. I hope I get an invite to it." I say with a laugh.

"Of course, I would love to have you there."

She leaves to find her seat with Clive and I go to see if I can find Ashley before she goes on the runway but I can't seem to find her anywhere. I look backstage to see if I can see her but I can't seem to find her, there is too much movement going on. Models are still getting dressed, the smell of hairspray is so strong, I can almost taste it. Models are getting their dresses fitted, some are in chairs having final touches to their makeup but I still can't find Ashley.

I check outside, near the bins to see if she has come outside, even though it's nighttime, the air is still a little warm but there is a breeze. I look around but she is nowhere so I am just about to head back inside when I hear a voice behind me.

"Did you really think you would get away with stealing from me?" That voice was so familiar. I turned around and saw Roxy standing there, wearing a red dress, with a long white coat over it.

"What are you doing here?" I ask but I don't care.

"I'm here to make sure that everyone knows that you stole my designs."

"You mean, you stole my designs." I argued back.

"Jake, come on, let's be honest, whose designs were they?" she says in a patronising tone.

"Are you being serious? You know that they are my designs, you just wanted them for yourself so you could take the credit because you haven't designed anything yourself for a long time and tonight I have just found out that I was not the first person you have done this too." I admit.

"What do you mean?" She is trying to sound innocent but I can see straight through this act she is putting on.

"You have stolen the designs from another one of your apprentices, who is currently inside right now and she has told me all about you." The look of guilt that spreads over her face was priceless, she had no idea I knew about that.

"No…no I didn't" she stutters "only yours."

"So you admit it then, you stole my designs."

As I looked at her face, it was like I could tell what was going on in her brain, trying to look for an excuse to come up with to get her out of this situation but unfortunately for her, she couldn't come up with one. "Fine, maybe I stole a few designs but it was just for inspiration, I would never have used the actual design."

"What a bunch of crap!" I shouted. I had officially had enough of her now. "You stole the whole collection of another person and passed it off as your own and now you want me to believe that you wouldn't have done the same thing to me and my designs."

"I wouldn't have, I would have used them only for inspiration."

"Yeah I'm sure you would have." I replied sarcastically. "You know what I actually feel sorry for you, the fact that you have to steal other peoples designs and take the credit means you have no ideas of your own, you have to steal them off others and that's very sad. I'm not angry at you, I feel sorry for you." I turn to open the door and I can hear the music faintly coming from the event. "Just go home, Roxy."

I was just about to walk off when she said "I will tell everyone how you stole my designs and no one will ever buy from you."

"If that is what you feel that you need to do, you do it but you will never have my designs, now if you'll excuse me I have a fashion show to attend." I am just about to walk off when I stop myself and turn to her. "Remember the number one rule in this industry, people in this business only lookout for themselves." I watch the door close on her.

I walked back to the studio where the show was being held. Everyone is still having a good time, no one has noticed I have been gone at all which is a good thing and Selena is taking care of everything as she said she would. I go to my dressing room to get my jacket on. I got my suit which was a gift from Clive, a dark grey suit and I didn't put the jacket on as I didn't need it but after being outside I was a little cold. The dressing room wasn't a big room but it was big enough for me, a sofa, dressing table with a mirror and a rack with a few outfit options for me but I already knew I was wearing the suit that Clive gave me.

I sat down at the table and looked in the mirror, trying to give myself just a few minutes of peace and quiet before I had to go out. I could still hear the music and noises coming from outside but with the door closed, it was very faint. I put my head in my hands just for a minute and looked down at the table in front of me when I heard the door open.

"Just need a few minutes Selena." I heard the door close but I didn't hear her say anything back so I looked up and there behind me, he was staring at me "dad."

Chapter 16

For a few seconds he just stared at me. I didn't know what else to say. Out of all the people that I was going to see tonight, I didn't think he was going to be one of them. I just didn't expect to see him tonight or ever again.

I turned around on my chair to face him. I could feel my heart beat faster but I wasn't going to let him know that I was scared, I wasn't going to give him the satisfaction of knowing that he can still scare me.

"What are you doing here?" I asked, trying to sound confident.

"I saw one of your invites and it had this address on it so I thought I would come and see you."

I was surprised that he even found me but to actually come to a fashion show I was astonished.

"So what are you doing here?" I ask again.

"I've come here to tell you that I'm sorry and you need to come home."

"Why would I do that?" I look at him confused.

He walks over to the sofa, unbuttons his jacket to sit down. "I think it's time you gave up this silly dream of yours and come home." He states.

I sat in silence for a few seconds, he still thinks that this is just a silly dream and has never taken this seriously nor will he ever take it seriously.

"This isn't some silly dream of mine, this is exactly what I should be doing. For the first time in my life I'm happy." I stare at him waiting for his response.

He stays quiet, he looks around the dressing room and I just know he is finding something wrong with it.

"I think you have made your point, this was a little phase you were going through but now it's time to be serious and start learning the business."

"No." I say with a slightly higher voice.

"Look, if it's about your brothers bullying you then I have told them and they both have promised me that they will not do it ever again."

I thought about my brothers and how much I hadn't missed them since I had been gone. I don't have any happy memories of all of us as there is none, well none for me to remember. All I remember is the beatings, name calling, getting locked in rooms and them laughing on the other side of the door.

"Do you really think that if I came back home, that it wouldn't go back to how it was?"

"No, because I have told them what they did was wrong and they are sorry for what they did."

"Yeah of course they are." I reply sarcastically.

"They really are sorry, they actually miss you."

"No they dont, they miss someone to bully daily." I state another fact.

"That's not true, you have always been more sensitive than them but they have promised me that they will stop it."

"Even if they are sorry and it doesn't go back to how it was, what makes you think I would even go back."

"Because like it or not we are your family and families stick together."

I laugh out loud not because what he has just said is funny but because I know that he is being serious.

"Families stick together do they?"

"Of course."

"So please tell me why you are here, trying to get me to come home and not sticking by me through my fashion show." I look straight in his eyes. He was just about to speak when I carried on talking. "Or why didn't you ever say anything to Leo and Liam when they would bully me? Why didn't you comfort us when mum died? Why were you always so interested in the business instead of taking care of your family!" I bawled at him.

He stands up so fast and gets so close to my face. "I WAS GRIEVING!"

"SO WAS I!" I shouted back.

We lock eye contact before he sits back down on the sofa and I go to put my jacket on which was hanging up on the rack of clothes. "It doesn't matter anymore, I'm not coming home so you are just going to have to deal with it."

I am just about to walk out of the room when he grabs my arm whilst still sitting down. "Your mum would be ashamed of you." his grip tight on my arm.

I lean down, look him straight in the eyes and quietly say "no, she would be ashamed of you." he stares at me, shocked by what I have just said.

"If you walk out that door, I will hit you so hard you won't even be able to see your precious fashion show."

"If that's what it takes for you to feel like a man then do it." After I said it I knew that I would never forgive him. Family for him is all about who he can control and he is only happy when you fall in line and family shouldn't be like that, it should be about love and loving your children not bullying them into what you want them to do. I shrug to get him off me, when he finally lets me go I slam the door behind me.

My heart is beating so fast and hard right now and even though I am happy I can feel my eyes start to water. Selena who I see is walking towards me. "There you are, where have you been?" she asks whilst talking to someone on her phone.

I didn't want to tell her the truth so I just made an excuse that I needed the toilet.

We both walked until we reached backstage. I peeked around the corner to have a look at the crowd and the place was full, there were only a few people standing as most were now in their seats, waiting for the show to begin.

"You ready?" Selena asked me.

"Yeah." I was ready but I was still nervous, everything that I had been through had all been leading to this moment.

The models were ready looking absolutely stunning in the dresses that I had created.

"Two minutes." I heard Selena say through her headset.

I walked down the line of models, smiling and telling them how great they all looked and there at the end, the last model was Ashley wearing in my opinion the best dress out of the whole collection.

"Hey."

"Hey I was looking for you." she tells me.

" I was looking for you, we might have just missed each other." She smiles at me. "You look amazing." I didn't think it was possible for her to look more remarkable but in that dress somehow she did.

"Thanks." she smiles.

Selena comes up behind me. "Jake, we are ready." she pulls me away before I have a chance to say goodbye.

I'm now waiting for the show to start. I take a few deep breaths and wait.

The music goes off, the lights turn down, I see the white runway light up, the photographers are there to make sure they get their perfect shot, the guests stop their conversations as they know the show is starting, the screens come to life with different patterns almost dancing and turning colours, Selena's idea and it was a good one to have.

The music starts with a soft melody, Fran, who is our first model. She is wearing a black jumpsuit with a sequin jacket and the shoes that she finally found. She walks out on that runway like she was born to do it, the photographers are going crazy, trying to get the perfect angle. I can see a few of the women who are wearing sunglasses remove them so they can see the outfit properly. I smile.

As the show goes on and more models are going out there, the less pressure I am feeling. I look over to where Clive is sitting with his two dates and Louise is sitting next to them, all four of them can't take their eyes off the runway.

Everyone seems to be enjoying the show, so far, none of the models have tripped or even stumbled which was a big fear of mine but so far it has been a perfect show. The only thing I have got to worry about is my walk that I have to make after everyone has seen the whole collection. I know that not all designers do it but I really want to. It's a fashion designer's way of saying 'thank you' to everyone who helped.

Ashley was the last one to walk the runway, when Lily came off the runway, Ashley knew it was her time. She smiled at her as she passed and took a deep breath, smiled at me then walked out. The lights turned red as she walked out. She stood for a second to pose, allowed for the photographers to get a photo of her then she continued to walk. I saw a few of the guests whisper to one another as soon as they saw the outfit. I knew they wanted it. A few of the younger guests were taking out their phones to film Ashley in the dress and hopefully post it on all their social media accounts.

Ashley reached the end of the runway and walked back, still not smiling which I know for her, that is really difficult to do but she managed it. She reached the end and disappeared from the crowd, so I hugged her, the smell of her perfume was sweet like vanilla. "You were amazing." I say proudly.
"Thanks." she says with a huge smile on her face. All the other models are waiting nearby to go and do the last walk of the show. Ashley makes her way to the end of the line as she was the last model to walk out.
As soon as the models start walking out in a single file on the runway, I can hear the applause and I can hear the cheering. All the models are

now standing at both sides of the runway and now it's my turn to walk out there.

My heart is beating so fast, my palms are sweaty and my mouth is so dry but at the same time I can't wait to go out there and take the credit not just for my collection but for everything that I have been through to get to this moment.

As soon as I stood out from behind the screen that was hiding me, the applause got louder. I saw the whole audience stand on their feet, still clapping and cheering. From this viewpoint the room looks so different, it's like I am looking at the whole room for the first time.

I am looking out to the crowd, I see Clive who is now standing, raising his champagne glass to me and I smile back at him. I look at both sides of me and the models are clapping for me with huge smiles on their faces.

I look around and everyone and I am just taking it all in. I never want to forget this feeling. I take a bow. I feel calmer now, it's like all the anxiety and pressure have finally gone and I'm just enjoying the moment. This is nothing like my dream, this feels so much better.

I am looking out in the crowd when I notice my dad, he stayed for the whole fashion show. He looks at me but it's not with happiness or even contentment, it was a look of disgust and disappointment, we made eye contact and then he walked out of the door.

"Who was that?" Ashley asked who was standing near me.

"My past." I say with a smile.

The show had finally ended, the models were backstage getting dressed and I was talking to Clive when Selena came over to us. "Jake, I would like to introduce you to someone." The woman who she was standing with was in her early 50s, short black hair, tanned skin and the whitest teeth I have ever seen. "This is Fleur Davenport, she is the CEO of Kleren."

"Oh wow, erm hello." I am in total shock. Kleren is one of the most recognizable names on the highstreet, there are about 100 stores worldwide and now the woman behind the brand is talking to me.

"My mum used to love to shop at your stores." I remember my mum would spend so many hours in these stores, trying on dresses and looking like a million pounds.

"Thank you so much." Is she here tonight?" she asks and everyone goes quiet.

"No, she passed away a few years ago."

"I'm so sorry." she said apologetically.

"It's fine, you didn't know." She looked like wanted the ground to open up and for her to disappear. "Did you enjoy the show?" I ask in an attempt to change the subject.

"I did indeed, so much so that I wonder if you would be interested in having your whole collection in my stores." she said it so nonchalantly that I thought I had misheard her.

"What, you…want...my designs?" I stuttered.

"I love the collection, I think it's just what the ideal Kleren's customer wants right now, something new, something fresh, so what do you say?" I am speechless, the words are in my head but my mouth is not saying anything, no noise is coming out at all. I'm just surprised. I can't believe this is happening. "I'll tell you what I will do, I will give you my card and you can call me in a few days with an answer." She hands me a small card and leaves.

Ashley comes over and hugs me, as she has overheard the conversation and is so happy for me. "I can't believe that has just happened."

"I know, it's incredible."

"So are you going to call her?"

"Of course but for now I just want to enjoy the rest of my night."

THE END

Printed in Great Britain
by Amazon